THE LAST MAN

THE WESLEYAN

EARLY CLASSICS OF

SCIENCE FICTION

SERIES

GENERAL EDITOR

ARTHUR B. EVANS

JEAN-BAPTISTE FRANÇOIS

XAVIER COUSIN DE GRAINVILLE

Translated by I. F. *&* M. CLARKE

Introduction & Critical Material by

I. F. CLARKE

Wesleyan University Press   Middletown, Connecticut

Last Man

Published by Wesleyan University Press,

Middletown, CT 06459

Translation and critical materials © 2002 by I. F. Clarke and M. Clarke

All rights reserved

Printed in the United States of America

ISBN 0-8195-6549-0 cloth

ISBN 0-8195-6608-X paper

Design by Richard Hendel

Set in Carter & Cone Galliard and Emigre Mason type

by B. Williams & Associates, Durham, N.C.

5   4   3   2   1

Cataloging-in-Publication Data appear on the last printed page of the book.

Title-page illustration: [detail] Octave Saunier, *Paris en ruines* (1893).

CONTENTS

ILLUSTRATIONS

Octave Saunier, *Paris en ruines* (1893)

PREFACE

There are good reasons for thinking that the first tale of the Last Man was *Le Dernier Homme,* written by Jean-Baptiste François Xavier Cousin de Grainville, published posthumously in French in 1805 and in English translation in 1806. The present new translation of that seminal science fiction work owes much to the help and advice of many people here in the United Kingdom, the United States, and France. We wish to express our gratitude to all who have helped us in the task of translating and editing the original story — from the first fraught moments when we realized it would not be possible to recycle that first and only English translation. We thank Dr. Arthur B. Evans of DePauw University and Suzanna Tamminen of Wesleyan University Press for their careful oversight of our labors and especially for the calm with which they responded to the news that the 1806 English text was far from satisfactory.

As the work advanced, we relied greatly on the help of libraries, especially the London Library and the Bodleian Library. Our grateful thanks to all there who never failed to deliver the books we needed. There were also occasional problems related to late-eighteenth-century French terminology and the history of France — all of them rapidly resolved on the Internet by Bernard Cazes of *Politique Étrangère,* Marc Madouraud of *Le Bulletin des Amateurs d'Anticipation Ancienne,* and Xavier Legrand-Ferronnière, editor of *Le Visage Vert* And for all queries about emblems and images, we never failed to have rapid answers from Dr. Robert Dingley of the University of New South Wales. Our grateful thanks to all of them.

Now, as prelude to this new translation of the first French edition of *Le Dernier Homme,* there first needs to be an account of the original English version of 1806 — a tale of two cities, two publishers,

LE
DERNIER HOMME,

OUVRAGE POSTHUME;

PAR M. DE GRAINVILLE,

HOMME DE LETTRES.

TOME I.

A PARIS,

Chez **DETERVILLE**, Libraire, rue du
Battoir, n° 16, quartier S. André-des-Arcs.

AN XIV — 1805.

THE
LAST MAN,

OR

OMEGARUS

AND

𝕾𝖞𝖉𝖊𝖗𝖎𝖆,

A ROMANCE IN FUTURITY.

IN TWO VOLUMES.

Through what new scenes and changes must we pass ?—
The wide, th'unbounded, prospect lies before me.—

ADDISON'S CATO.

VOL. I

LONDON:

PRINTED FOR R. DUTTON, 45,
GRACECHURCH-STREET.

1806.

and some unseemly literary practices. A comparison of the title pages of the original French text and of this anonymous translation is instructive. *The Last Man; or, Omeragus and Syderia: A Romance in Futurity* had appeared with great speed, some ten months after the posthumous publication of the French edition of 1805. Clearly designed to reinforce the impression of a wholly British work, the title is very different from the one that appeared in the original French version. The name of Grainville, prominent in the French, does not appear on the title page of what purports to be an English-language first edition; there was nothing to suggest that the primary text had not been first written in English. Indeed, the artful epigraph from Addison's *Cato* — most English of authors — was undoubtedly intended to add to the appearance of homespun, native authenticity. Nevertheless, it is important to note that this English version of 1806 is a veritable minefield of errors and contains a multitude of serious professional fouls.

The present translation of Grainville's *Le Dernier Homme* is a necessary replacement for that first defective text of *The Last Man*. We now know the latter to be an anonymous and pirated English version of the French original — the first major instance of brazen publisher deceit in the history of future fiction. This English translation was cited under "Anonymous" in the first edition of my bibliography *The Tale of the Future* (Library Association, 1961), where it was classified with the other entries ("published in the United Kingdom between 1644 and 1960") as a British text by an unknown English author. In those early days, I knew that Pierre Versins was then working on his monumental *Encyclopédie de l'Utopie, des Voyages extraordinaires et de la Science-Fiction* and, with prodigious energy, was scanning all sources for information on authors and topics that had any connection with his research. In 1962, Pierre wrote to ask me: "Does the first sentence in the first chapter of *The Last Man* give the English for — 'Proche les ruines de Palmyre, il est un antre solitaire si redouté des Syriens qu'ils l'ont appelé la caverne de la mort'?" I replied to say that the two were indeed totally equivalent. And back came the surprising news that the presumed English publication of *The Last Man* was undoubtedly an unacknowledged translation of *Le Dernier Homme* by Jean-Baptiste François Xavier Cousin de Grainville. "La bibliographie," Pierre wrote, "me donne le cauchemar" ("Bibliography gives me nightmares").

For many years I had good reason to think, like many others, that *The Last Man* was the English title that was entered under "Anonymous" in the catalogs of the British Library and the Bodleian Library and in the *National Union Catalog* of the United States — an early example of future fiction in English, author unknown. After Pierre Versins had revealed the identity of the work's true author, I subsequently assumed that the translation was a faithful English-language version of *Le Dernier Homme*. In *The Pattern of Expectation, 1644–2001* (1979), for example, I even cited one passage as a telling example of the rapid transfer of new scientific ideas to fiction. It seemed quite conclusive to say that a few years after 1798 — the year when Edward Jenner published his *Inquiry into the Causes and Effects of the Variolae Vaccinae* and Thomas Malthus raised momentous questions about the future in his *Essay on the Principle of Population* — Grainville had set down his reasons for expecting the inevitable end of the human race. These reasons found more than sufficient explanation in the writings of Jenner and Malthus, since Grainville clearly pointed to "the profound improvements making in medical science, by which the lives of thousands of the infantine world have been snatched from the empire of death, and who, in thus becoming the heads of numerous progenies, are laying the foundation of an immense population which the earth in after-ages will be inadequate to sustain."[1]

Unfortunately, as I now realize, these lines did not appear in the original French edition. These striking phrases were invented by the translator. They were inserted into the narrative in order, it seems, to strengthen the brief passage on the same page where, as Grainville wrote, it was recognized from the beginning that "the duration of human life was wisely regulated by the omniscient mind of the Almighty, according to the size of the globe and the fecundity of its inhabitants."

The discovery of the interpolated passage came soon after I had begun what I thought would be a rapid reading of the French original. I turned to my wife for assistance, and together we made our way through a detailed comparison of both the French and English versions. That was the beginning of our collaboration. Our close reading revealed a succession of unexpected and interesting discrepancies between the two texts. First, we found that the anonymous translator had rearranged the book for reasons that had nothing to do with literature. The Grainville version follows the epic style: division into ten *Chants,* which are self-contained major sections of the narrative. In the English version, these are replaced by a division into twenty-one chapters, presumably designed to give *A Romance in Futurity* the appearance of the everyday London fiction to be found in the circulating libraries.[2] Next, we soon found frequent evidence of serious mistranslations and of extraordinary failures in idiom.

In the end, we arrived at the following inescapable conclusion: a page-by-page comparison of *Le Dernier Homme* and *The Last Man* suggests that the many errors in the English translation came from a person who was not a native English speaker. The translation proceeds satisfactorily enough for three to four pages on average and then collapses into a black hole of misinterpretations. For example, *une negligence distraite* (bk. 2, p. 110) appears as "an absent negligence" (vol. 2, p. 124). Again, "mature the granivorous harvest" (1:46), offered as the translation of *dorer les moissons* (1:49), betrays a surprising error in translation and basic unfamiliarity with English idioms.[3]

A comparable failure in idiom is the translation of *Si mes récoltes n'ont pas payé mes sueurs avec usure* (1:50), which is rendered as "If my harvests have not repaid my labors with usury" (1:54). In modern English, the idiomatic phrase remains the same as it was in 1806: "repay with interest" — one of many slips that we read as evidence of an alien hand. What English-French dictionary would ever give "Grand Priest" (2:150), as the correct rendering of *Grand-prêtre* (2:131)? Surely, we thought, only a translator with a less than perfect knowledge of English could have transformed *On se disoit à soi-même*

(1:130) into the absurd "We internally said" (1:142). Additional examples of such basic errors in translation include the following: *vécu dans le présent* (1:3) as "always lived in his present retreat" (1:3); *quels grands spectacles* (1:76) as "what admirable deportment" (1:80); and *Cette tempête s'appaise* (1:123) as "the storm appeased" (1:136).

Failings of this kind were also aggravated by serious omissions in the text. For example, the translator seems to have sought wherever possible to reduce the French element — especially in those accounts and episodes that Grainville had intended for the greater glory of his own countrymen. Out went phrases, sentences, and even paragraphs favorable to the French; and, on one notable occasion, three entire pages vanished from the original. English readers would never know that the missing pages were an elaborate exultation of French achievements and a fulsome tribute to "that great man called Napoleon I."[4] This kind of tactical editing made good business sense in 1806, the year after the decisive naval victory at Trafalgar, when patriotic feelings were still running high in the United Kingdom. This element of purposeful calculation — the deliberate concealment of French references, the suppression of French authorship, and the absence of "Translated from the French" — necessarily led us to the following verdict: this was obviously a case of literary piracy for immediate profit by a person, possibly persons, unknown.

The profit motive so evident in this criminal enterprise of 1806 is a telling indication of the growing international interest in tales of the future. The first futuristic utopia in English, *The Reign of George VI* (1763), was translated into German. Sébastien Mercier's far more famous *L'An 2440* (1771) had an English translation in 1772, and it inspired some seven imitations (in German, Dutch, and Danish) between 1777 and 1792. Although Grainville's *Le Dernier Homme* was quickly translated into English, the original did not at first enjoy any comparable success in France. This failure in popularity was a national scandal to Charles Nodier, who edited the second edition of 1811.[5] "The fate of this work," he wrote in his preface, "astonished me. The first edition was launched in obscurity — not a single reviewer, not a single man of letters deigned to advocate it in the face of public indifference." (See the appendix, in which Nodier's preface is given in full.) Nodier then introduced a surprising English connection, presenting Sir Herbert Croft to his French readers as a most perceptive admirer of Grainville. Croft had apparently commented on *Le Dernier Homme* "with an enthusiasm that does honor to both of them."

The rest of this story belongs to the introduction, where we follow the history of Grainville's *Le Dernier Homme* through its various transformations. His singular story was the first tale of the future to consider the death of all human beings and the destruction of the earth — a Last Day acted out in accordance with the will of God. Grainville's tale of global apocalypse was perhaps the first in this genre, but it would be far from the last. One hundred and forty years later, after Hiroshima, the greatest flood of apocalyptic fiction would begin; and, throughout the ensuing four decades, a seemingly endless succession of books and films would describe the End of the World as the last act in a chain of human follies.

I. F. Clarke & M. Clarke
Milton under Wychwood

INTRODUCTION

"This is the Way the World will End"

The Closing, The Doom, The Flame Deluge, The Happening, The Leveling, The Rat Bomb Wars, The War of a Thousand Suns, World War Terminus, Zero Day — these are some of the many names that recall the last days of the Old People in the hundreds of stories that once told the tale of a world returned to dust. *After Doomsday, Death of a World, The Last Day, Earthwreck, World in Eclipse* — these are the uncompromising titles that foretold the worst of all possible futures for all people on earth.[1] They described, and some striking films showed, the last desolate days after the flash in the sky — ominous images, like the end scene of the mushroom cloud in *Dr. Strangelove* and the dark atomic cloud in *On the Beach*. These have shown the world how those who live by the Bomb shall surely perish by the Bomb.

These projected disasters are recent entries in the brief history of future fiction. They are a positive moral response to the greatest peril of modern times — the dangerous imbalance between human society and the ever-increasing genocidal capacity of military weapons. The ghost of Frankenstein greatly troubled the second half of the twentieth century, for there were good reasons to fear that one day science could produce monsters, as Gore Vidal showed in *Kalki* (1978). His theme is the unmaking of mankind, the mad dream of wiping out all human beings save for the chosen few who are to re-create human society. Earth becomes a shadow theater for this last play about the uses and the abuses of the sciences. As the lethal virus *Yersinia enterocolitica* finishes off all but the last five people on planet earth, Gore Vidal presents his postscript to Mary Shelley's *Frankenstein*, an epitaph for the human race written in the last hours of the final catastrophe: "When the dance of eternity ended, the age of Kali began. Four billion or so men, women, children died. Not all at once. Some may have survived for as long as a week. We shall never know for certain. In most cases death was swift — a matter of seconds, minutes, a mercifully unconscious hour."[2]

All that follows will seek to show that these visions of the last days of Earth are the end story in the tale of the future — the one occasion when fiction has the last possible word about our species and the future of our world. These histories of the catastrophe-to-come are quite distinct in mood and intention from all other accounts of coming things. They have their own dedicated roles and separate evolutionary patterns within the tale of the future, that great *omnium gatherum* of the most diverse stories that only have the future tense in common. The various modes in this speculative literature have established the tale of the future as a most appropriate mediator between technological society and those many potential factors — social, political, military, and scientific — that could possibly change a nation, a continent, or the whole world for better or for worse. From the earliest anticipations in the eighteenth century, the tale of the future has been all things to all writers. The great variety of these stories reveals how matter is forever seeking its proper literary form in projections about the course and consequences of a future war, or the journey to other worlds in space, or the society of the future, or the limitless possibilities of science fiction, or that ultimate conjecture — the last will and testament of the human race — in accounts of the Last Man and the end of our world.

Adaptation is the power that energizes these tales of coming things; and their evolutionary capacity for rapid change has, from time to time, transformed the manner and the message of the final disaster story in keeping with the calculus of possibilities. Since 1918, and most of all since 1945, the Preacher has prophesied that the collapse of society, even the end of all life on earth, will follow from some act of human folly. Aldous Huxley, for example, put humanity on trial in his *Ape and Essence* (1949). In the year 2108, in the blasted wastelands of Southern California, the Arch-Vicar of Belial takes the text for his homily on Progress and Nationalism from the undisputed fact that "technological progress provides people with the instruments of ever more indiscriminate destruction."[3] Ten years after that, in a more forceful and original story, Walter Miller gave the world a second chance in *A Canticle for Leibowitz* (1959), one of the classic tales of the final disaster. His story opens in the long Dark Ages that follow a nuclear war. Civilized society returns — only to repeat the cycle of discovery and destruction. Another war, another end scene for the human race, as the last starship with its load of children sets off for the planets. The horizon becomes a red glow. *Sic transit mundus!*

The spaceship was often the Ark of salvation for the chosen few who are to survive the destruction of our planet. That small hope met total rejection, however, in the 103 Songs of the long poem *Aniara* (1956). There, the Swedish poet Harry Martinson wrote an epitaph for the eight thousand emigrants on the "goldonda" *Aniara*, lost far out in deep space, seeking refuge in the planets from a devastated world. In the "final ebbing hours of human time" they realize that, like their society, they have lost their way:

I had coveted a Paradise for this race
but since we left the one we had destroyed
the Zodiac's lonely light became our only home,
a gaping chasm in which no god could hear us.

The eternal mystery of Heaven's stars,
The miracle of the celestial mechanism,
Is the law but not the Gospel.
Mercy can only thrive where there is life.[4]

Before the First World War, these tales of the last days generally had no warnings for feckless mortals. They offered a choice of futures: either meditations on the inevitable course of nature — for it was written that the world would come to an end — or survival stories about the struggle for existence in the hard time after Day Zero. One remarkable variation on this theme came from the English writer M. P. Shiel, who first-footed the twentieth century with *The Purple Cloud* (1901). Exit the entire human race save for the solitary and half-demented but necessary survivor. In those days the only candidates for survival were men, and the second Adam sets off to roam the world, burning everything he fancies as he moves from country to country, "like some being of the Pit that blights where his wings of fire pass . . . I have burned Calcutta, Pekin, and San Francisco . . . Like Leviathan disporting himself in the sea, so I have rioted in the earth."[5]

Fantastic scenes and prodigious activity, but they cannot compare with the quiet tone and steady pace of the narrative in H. G. Wells's *The Time Machine* (1895), when the Time Traveller reports on the end of old Terra as he saw it happening. A century later, his account is still the most moving and most convincing description of its kind, for Wells sends the Traveller speeding through the millennia, the Last Man on his way to see the last days of our world. He travels ever onwards ". . . stopping ever and again, drawn on by the mystery of earth's fate, watching with a strange fascination the sun grow larger and duller in the westward sky, and the life of old earth ebb away. At last, more than thirty million years hence, the huge red-hot dome of the sun had come to obscure nearly a tenth part of the darkling heavens . . . I looked about to see if any traces of animal life remained. A certain indefinable apprehension still kept me in the saddle of the machine. But I saw nothing moving, in earth or sky or sea. The green slime on the rocks alone testified that life was not extinct."[6]

Ninety years before that end-of-the-century spectacle, the Last Man made his first appearance in speculative fiction. His history begins in France with the posthumous publication in 1805 of *Le Dernier Homme* by Jean-Baptiste François Xavier Cousin de Grainville, and it is continued in 1826 with Mary Shelley's *The Last Man*. These singular, very different narratives followed on, but owed nothing to, earlier stories of the future, as a comparison with the first utopias of the future will make clear.[7] In the early formative period of future fiction, long before Félix Bodin made the first study of *la littérature futuriste* in his survey of the new fiction in *Le Roman de l'avenir* (1834), the original time travelers had to make their own ways through the uncharted area of the future without benefit of guides or maps. Indeed, Grainville had not yet presented himself as a candidate for the priesthood when the first detailed and prescriptive utopia of the future appeared in England. The author of *The Reign of George VI, 1900–1925* (1763) remains unknown, but his message from the year 1763 comes through loud and clear: monarchy is the best form of government.

In this story, there will be no technological changes in the twentieth century. (What could they foresee in 1763?) This first ideal state of the future is a literary fossil from long ago; for the author wrote in the last years before the great political and mechanical revolutions of the late eighteenth century would abolish kingly power in some countries and would offer independence for all from the immemorial limitations of horsepower, the windmill, and the waterwheel. In fact, the author had such faith in his steady-state expectations that he presented his narrative as a continuing chronicle of the British people and their kings. It opens briefly in real time with the restoration of the Stuart monarchy in 1660 and then rapidly moves on into a future history, "taken up at a what's-to-come period and begun at an aera that will not begin these hundred years."[8]

What was the shape of the future in 1763? The most desirable political transformation of Europe would come about by applying the theories of government that the author borrowed from the *Idea of a Patriot King* (1749), a propaganda tract written by that ardent monarchist Viscount Bolingbroke. His program for the future of his country can be summarized as follows: successful wars and a successful monarch. For twenty years, George VI is engaged in conducting military campaigns. This wish-fulfillment fantasy has him defeating the major European powers of that time one after the other — Austria, France, Russia, Spain — and by 1920 he has become king of France. In that *annus mirabilis,* there was good news from "the immense region which the English possessed in North America." Like a latter-day Ozymandias, the author sees the future as a wagon train rolling on forever toward the promised land of world empire:

> The King was there sovereign of a tract of much greater extent than all Europe. The constitution of the several divisions of that vast monarchy was admirably designed to keep the whole in continual dependance on the mother country. There were eleven millions of souls in the British American dominions in the year 1920: they were in possession of perhaps the finest country in the world, and yet had never made the least attempt to shake off the authority of Great Britain. Indeed, the multiplicity of governments which prevailed over the whole country — the various constitutions of them, rendered the execution of such a scheme absolutely impossible.[9]

The tale of the future can never stand still. The theories, hopes, and fears of today are always in waiting to enact their versions of tomorrow's drama. So, eight years after the celebration of kingship in the *Reign of George VI*, it was the turn for French ideas about democracy and parliamentary government to reveal what could be accomplished for the improvement of the world. In fact, Sébastien Mercier's *L'An 2440* brought such good news that the book became the first instant success in future fiction: eleven editions between 1771 and 1799, four English translations, two American editions (copies in the libraries of George Washington and Thomas Jefferson), and translations into Dutch, German, and Italian, plus many imitations.[10] The France of the year 2440 is a happy country, transformed by the ideas of Montesquieu, Voltaire, and Rousseau. The undeclared slogans for this new age are liberty and equality, freedom of thought, universal education, and constitutional monarchy — not for France alone but for the whole world. Mercier has the glory of first introducing the promise of life without frontiers; for all the peoples of his world live in peace, and all the kings "have made their glory consist in governing wisely, wishing rather to cause the happiness of a small number than to gratify the frenzied ambition of ruling over desolated countries filled with aching hearts."[11]

Mercier made a second contribution to the tale of the future in his revised edition of 1786 when he added a new chapter, "L'Aéro-stat." It was an important addition, since it contained the first major extrapolation from a new technology to future achievement. Mercier looked forward from the recent balloon ascents in Paris to the prospects of intercontinental aviation. He had witnessed, and later wrote about, the first successful manned balloon ascent on 21 November 1783, when Pilâtre de Rozier and the marquis d'Arlandes took off in their Montgolfier balloon from the garden of the Château de la Muette. Benjamin Franklin was there, watching with a telescope from the terrace of his house in Passy. The extraordinary sight of the two men he could see traveling through the air later moved him to predict that the balloon would someday become a military weapon — airborne attacks by "ten thousand troops descending from the skies."[12] Not so for Mercier. His new chapter, "L'Aérostat," opened with the arrival of an immense flying machine, the courier from Pekin; and he goes on to describe the coming advances in world unity and in world communications that would follow on the achievements of the aeronauts, "moving from one climate to another in twenty-four hours, traversing distances that used to separate the most distant countries."[13]

Balloons of great size and speed, transported by hot air or hydrogen, became a favorite marker in future fiction — an unmistakable indicator of coming things. Grainville, for instance, made great play with his "ships of the air" in the second canto of *Le Dernier Homme*, where Omegarus relates the preparations for an aerial journey across the Atlantic:

The capital of Normandy had for a long time been one of the most famous points of departure for ships of the air. In the many stores of the city, there were still containers filled with those volatile spirits that could carry men above the clouds more powerfully than the sails of ships or the wings of birds. Idamas had already brought these containers to the assembly point. Already the subtle ether was filling out the airship which swayed about, eager for take-off. I looked on with keen interest at a sight which I had never experienced before. The globe especially attracted my attention. On the stern, written in letters of gold, were the words *I have made the journey round the world.*

The first readers of *Le Dernier Homme* must have been struck by the phrase "Ouvrage Posthume" on its title page. If they inquired about the last days of Grainville, they would have heard that he had committed suicide by throwing himself into the Somme Canal at Amiens about two o'clock in the morning on 1 February 1805 — a sad end to an unhappy life. Sensitive, imaginative, a dreamer, incapable of guile, often deceived — that was Jean-Baptiste François Xavier Cousin de Grainville, according to those who knew him.[14] Indeed, the brief story of his life reveals a personal element that the many histories of the Last Man confirm; for it is not surprising to find that tales of the catastrophe-to-come owe much to the life experience of their writers and are often linked with a contemporary mood of melancholy, even of fear and despair. Grainville certainly knew fear and despair. He was born in Le Havre in 1746, a child of the lesser nobility and a gifted student. He entered the seminary of Saint-Sulpice, was ordained priest, and became a pamphleteer, asserting the primacy of religious belief against *les philosophes* of the day. In 1790, Grainville took the oath to the Republic, as required by the Constituent Assembly, became a *prêtre constitutionnel,* and left the priesthood when the Terror came.[15] Later, he married but did not live happily ever after: there was little money, his circumstances were wretched, and there were few opportunities for him as a teacher. Late in January 1805, he fell ill with a fever, which worsened by the day, and then he was found dead in the canal in Amiens.

Grainville never achieved his lifelong ambition of writing an epic poem about the Last Man, as Charles Nodier explained in his preface to the second edition of *Le Dernier Homme,* published in 1811 (see the appendix). He had, however, already written his *poème en prose* in order to set down the whole story of the last days as a necessary preparation for his poetic version of "Things unattempted yet in Prose or Rhyme" (*Paradise Lost*, 1:16). No one had ever done what he planned; for the origin of his story is beyond time in the eternity of God's will, and the start of the action is the creation of man and the fall of Adam. Literary friends (Bernardin de Saint-Pierre, Charles Nodier, and others) who had seen this text urged Grainville to publish; but he died before he could see *Le Dernier Homme* through the press. That was done for him by Charles Nodier. Although no more than forty copies of the first edition were sold, Grainville had achieved a *succès d'estime*, for he had gained that respect, Nodier wrote, "which leads those of generous heart to insist on due recognition for an unfortunate and forgotten talent." He had his admirers. There was Sir Herbert Croft, antiquarian and linguist, who had all London talking in 1780 about his projected epitaphs in *The Abbey of Kilkhampton; or, Monumental Records for the Year 1980;* and there was Jules Michelet, eminent historian, who thought so highly of Grainville that he gave him a special place in his *Histoire du XIXe siècle*, holding him to be a more significant figure than Malthus. In his long, laudatory account of Grainville's life, Michelet noted that Krofft, as he called him, came to live in Amiens soon after the death of Grainville. Croft was "an English antiquarian and a tireless seeker after literary curiosities. He knew the *Dernier Homme*, and he asked eagerly to see the original and gifted creator of the work that he considered the only modern epic. Alas! He was no more. Krofft wept bitterly. 'Ah!' said he. 'I would have saved him!'"[16]

That was an early response to the mythmaking powers of the new tales of the future; for the Last Man stories of Grainville and Mary Shelley are similar insofar as they were part of a general European interest in, almost cult of, fallen empires and the end of civilization. Their differences, however, are profound. Mary Shelley's version of *The Last Man* followed on an English vogue for end-of-the-world poems like Byron's dramatic end-of-the-world vision in "Darkness" (1816) and for paintings like Joseph Gandy's "Architec-

Joseph Gandy, *Architectural Ruins: A Vision* (1798). By courtesy of the Trustees of Sir John Soane's Museum.

tural Ruins: A Vision" (1798), which showed the shattered dome of the Rotunda in the then-new Bank of England building. Her story evolves in phase with an entirely secular scenario. An accident of nature, and nothing but that accident, leaves Lionel Verney as the last survivor of humankind. It is very different in *Le Dernier Homme*. The story is Catholic in orientation and derives both authority and force from the end-of-the-world vision in the Book of Revelation. As a priest, Grainville would have delivered many sermons on the Four Last Things: Death and Judgment, Hell or Heaven — matters for serious contemplation, as St. Thomas More observed in his own *Quattuor Novissimis* (c. 1533). Moreover, he could expect his French readers to know the stages of the Last Day encoded in the *Dies Irae*, once sung or said at all masses for the dead. The opening lines in the translation by Thomas Babington Macaulay present the traditional sequence of events:

On that great, that awful day,
This vain world shall pass away.
Thus the sibyl sang of old,
Thus hath Holy David told.
There shall be a deadly fear
When the Avenger shall appear,
And unveiled before his eye
All the works of man shall lie.
Hark! To the great trumpet's tones
Pealing o'er the place of bones:
Hark! It waketh from their bed
All the nations of the dead,
In a countless throng to meet
At the eternal judgment seat.[17]

Grainville evidently had in mind the apocalyptic scenario in Revelation where a trumpet-like voice cries out to Saint John, saying, "Come up hither, and I will shew thee things which must be hereafter" (4:1), with John then serving as both witness to and as prophet of God's cleansing of the earth. Such biblical passages are mirrored, for example, in the beginning of the end in the eighth canto, when Omegarus "looked up to heaven with confidence" and "found consolation in the recollection of a God who controls the world. Let the angels sound the trumpet that is to awaken the dead, let the earth be destroyed and the light of the sun and the stars be extinguished — Omegarus could contemplate those sights with courage. He was worthy to witness the last day of the world."

The story in *Le Dernier Homme,* however, is no action replay of the episodes in Revelation. Indeed, there are few direct borrowings, for Grainville clearly thought it suited his purpose best to set his singular account of Omegarus and Syderia against a foreground of long-established expectations about the Day of Judgment and the End of the World. His timescale is the duration of the known universe. His history of the last days opens with the first sight of Adam at the gates of Hell, where "Heaven had condemned him to watch sinners entering the infernal regions — a torment he had endured since the beginning of the world" (canto IV). The story finishes and time comes to an end when "The earth shook, was blown out of orbit, and was torn apart" (canto X). Although the narrative is undoubtedly orthodox in outline, the many original episodes show that Grainville exploited every opportunity to compose his own fantasia on the ways of God with man. The exotic opening pages, enchanted mirrors, the succession of apparitions, the clouds of fire, the ever-changing course of events, the various deceptions practiced by the Spirit of Earth, and especially the troubled tale of Omegarus and Syderia — these elements created the first Gothic romance of Heaven and Earth.

In effect, Grainville wrote his own sequel to Genesis. In the biblical account, there was a primal pair and there was Satan; and in the future world of this latter-day story, there is a final pair: Omegarus, named for the Last Man, and Syderia, who is the Last Woman. "Be you the happy Eve to this new Adam," says Ormus, "I join you in an everlasting union" (canto V). The primal pair had transgressed in their different ways, yielding to the temptations of Satan. That was "Man's First Disobedience" in Milton's *Paradise Lost* (1667); and, as Nodier observes in his preface, the ultimate act of obedience in *Le Dernier Homme* was Grainville's way of linking "the end of all things with their beginning." The frequent parallels between *Paradise Lost* and *Le Dernier Homme* confirm what one would expect: Grainville took the English poem as a model. The solemn, often exalted language, the elaborate epic similes, the use of dreams to calm or arouse, the roles of Uriel and Ithuriel, the descriptions of Eve, Mother of Mankind — these are major similarities. The most striking parallel, however, is the vision of the dreadful futures given to Adam and Omegarus. In *Paradise Lost* they are "Visions ill foreseen!":

. . . Let no man seek
Henceforth to be foretold what shall befall
Him or his Children, evil he may be sure,
Which neither his foreknowing can prevent,

And he the future evil shall no less
In apprehension than in substance feel
Grievous to bear: but that care now is past,
Man is not whom to warn: those few escap't
Famine and anguish will at last consume. (II:770–78)

What Grainville's Last Man sees is "his hideous progeny, misshapen in form and cruel in disposition, making perpetual war on one another" (canto VII).

In the last days, Omegarus and Syderia have to face a test of their obedience, which is very different from the ban on "the Fruit of that Forbidden Tree," for God demands of the Last Man "the most painful sacrifice that the human heart could make" (canto I) for the greater good of the human race. Grainville rewrote the divine veto in keeping with the findings of Jenner and the theories of Malthus. There had to be a limit to human existence, as God had foreseen. It was evident that "the Almighty had set the term of human life in accordance with the size of the earth and the fecundity of its inhabitants; that, if this balance were to be upset, if men prolonged their youth, the earth would not be capable of supporting their too numerous descendants who would fight to the death for living space" (canto III). In this last drama of life and death, Grainville made a final adjustment to the received story by giving the role of "Th'infernal Serpent" to the Spirit of Earth. The supreme earth force plays the part of the deceiver: he is the controller of the material world seeking self-preservation by any means, acting always in steadfast opposition to the divine scheme for humankind. The Spirit of Earth acts as the fault line that runs through the story, causing serious damage and great dismay until almost the last moment. Then Syderia, in a vision, hears the High Priest say to her: "Omegarus rebelled against my last commands and against the will of Heaven; but, in leaving you, he has made full amends" (canto IX).

Grainville began as he meant to go on — in the surreal context of a world in dissolution and in the sustained setting of unexpected apparitions and mysterious revelations. He followed on (and borrowed from) *Les Ruines, ou Méditations sur les révolutions des empires,* first published by Constantin-François Volney in 1791. These meditations offered a philosophy of history that chimed perfectly with the contemporary interest in themes of the decline and fall of nations that developed during the second half of the eighteenth century in England and in France.[18]

Grainville inspired a faithful few who made their additions to the tale of the Last Man. In 1831, Auguste-François Creuzé de Lesser published his versification of Grainville's story in *Le Dernier Homme: Poème imité de Grainville,* which had variations on the original. The most ingenious was a plan by Ormus to escape the end of our world by taking off to find "a new earth in space beneath a new sun." There is no escape, however. Magnetic storms in deep space compel the wanderers to return home. Another version appeared in 1858, *Omégar, ou Le Dernier Homme: Proso-poésie dramatique de la fin des temps en douze chants* by Élise Gagne.[19]

In English writings about the Last Man and the end of the world during this period, there are no borrowings and no similarities that could reveal any debts to France. It was another country, across the Channel. The concept of last things was different, both in word and in image, for the earliest anticipations of desolation did not follow any apocalyptic sequence to the end of the world in the Grainville style. In 1769, for instance, long before Volney contemplated his ruins, the anonymous author of *Private Letters from an American in England to his Friends in America* was content to deliver a moral lesson on national failings by showing the United Kingdom run-down and desolate, in the last stages of a well-deserved decline. This demonstration of the "declension of empires" derived much of its power from a fascination with ruins that followed from the extraordinary images of the Roman past, especially *Le Vedute di Roma,* which Giovanni Battista Piranesi began publishing in 1745. These drawings offered eighteenth-century *cognoscenti* especially dramatic scenes from a theater of the Sublime. The Temple of Venus, like the Colosseum, were powerful icons. They looked to past greatness and caused the viewer to foresee another revolution, which would surely come in the eternal rise and fall of civilizations. It was an expectation that had the authority of the prophet Jeremiah. Zion is desolate, he laments, and the foxes walk upon it: "How doth the city sit solitary that was full of people — how she is become as a widow! — she that was great among the nations, and princes among the provinces, how she is become tributary" (Lamentations 1:1–2). So, the traveler from a foreign land became a familiar visitor to an England that has seen far, far better times. The first to arrive was the American in *Private Letters*. The anonymous author plunged straight into his shocking narrative of a great nation without hope, clearly expecting the reader to accept without hesitation a story that begins in 1899 with a letter. There, he describes the arrival of the American vessel in the Channel, where "most of the harbors are choaked up, so as not to afford a channel for anything but a cutter." Although the reasons for the rapid decline and fall of the United Kingdom compose an exemplary catalog of recent moral and political failings, this instance of *Britannia derelicta* also exhibits the workings of historical inevitability. "What shall we say of these amazing changes?" That is the first question, as the author begins to tell the reason why. The end-of-empire story opens with a well-known quotation from Ovid: "And corn grows now where Troy town stood"(*Heroides*, 1.1.2). That potent recollection is enough to establish the links between future decline and present failures:

The declensions of Empires, we may reason on what may be, from what has been the fate of so many much greater ones, are to be considered as natural causes: and, though a lack of industry and primitive economy, joined to predominant and universal luxury and dissipation, may hasten and push on the minute hand of their destruction faster, yet, as Lord Bolingbroke so well observes, "Kingdoms are mortal like those who compose them." They have their infancy, their youth, and, though care and temperance may postpone it a while, yet must the common catastrophe happen, when dotage and death shall long struggle which shall be predominant, but in the end, the contest is divided in favor of the latter.[20]

"The next Augustan age will dawn on the other side of the Atlantic," so Horace Walpole wrote on 24 November 1774; and he thought that one day, in the style of the Grand Tour, "some curious traveler from Lima will visit England and give a description of the ruins of St. Paul's, like the editions of Balbec and Palmyra."[21] The traveler proved a most persuasive moral agent — a silent witness to bygone glory, a woe-crier ever ready to pass judgment on the failings of a nation. For example, American travelers find cause to reflect on the lesson, by "Time's slow finger written in the dust," when they visit the ruins of London in Anna Laetitia Barbauld's *Eighteen Hundred and Eleven* (1811):

> Night, Gothic night, again may shake the plains
> Where Power is seated, and where Science reigns;
> England, the seat of arts, be only known
> By the grey ruin and the moldering stone;
> That Time may tear the garland from her brow,
> And Europe sit in dust, as Asia now.[22]

"I met a traveler from an antique land," so Shelley began "Ozymandias" (1818), the most famous of these severe judgments on human failure:

> Nothing beside remains. Round the decay
> Of that colossal wreck, boundless and bare
> The lone and level sands stretch far away.

That was the classic form: the telling contrast between then and now. The variant form aimed to illuminate the difference between today and tomorrow, as can be seen in the sonnet Horace Smith wrote in the company of Shelley on the evening of 27 December

1817. Smith had undoubtedly seen Shelley's "Ozymandias," then awaiting publication in the *Examiner* for January 1818, since he transferred
the Egyptian story to an English future setting. The poem was "On
a Stupendous Leg of Granite, Discovered Standing by Itself in the
Deserts of Egypt, with the Inscription Inserted Below."

> In Egypt's sandy silence, all alone
> Stands a gigantic Leg, which far off throws
> The only shadow that the Desert knows.
> "I am great Ozymandias," saith the stone,
> "The King of kings: this mighty city shows
> The wonders of my hand." The city's gone!
> Naught but the leg remaining to disclose
> The sight of that forgotten Babylon.
> We wonder, and some hunter may express
> Wonder like ours, when through the wilderness
> Where London stood, holding the wolf in chase,
> He meets some fragment huge, and stops to guess
> What wonderful, but unrecorded, race
> Once dwelt in that annihilated place.[23]

By the first decade of the nineteenth century, the traveler had
found a place in the book of ready references and appropriate allu-
sions. By 1830, he was telling his tale at great length in a poem that
runs to sixty-one pages, *London in a Thousand Years,* by Eugenius
Roche:

> Here London stood, and gloried in her might . . .
> And lived in peace and joy — in wealth and guilt;
> Here I take up her burden, for 'tis mine;
> I am the lonely spirit of the past,
> Wand'ring mid wrecks and graves, and pouring forth
> My wailings in the desert. Babylon
> Where are thy merchants now — they dearest pride —
> The great men of the earth?[24]

By October 1840, the traveler had become the New Zealander, after Macaulay wrote in his review of Leopold von Ranke's *History of the Popes* of that future time "when some traveler from New Zealand shall, in the midst of a vast solitude, take his stand on a broken arch of London Bridge to sketch the ruins of St. Paul's." The New Zealander proved to be so useful an agent in fiction that he kept on reappearing. For instance, Henry O'Neil opened his admonitory account in *Two Thousand Years Hence* (1867) with a letter from Old London dated 31 December 3867. He began: "Dear Friend, Many years have elapsed since I left the lovely shores of New Zealand to undertake the magistracy of that district in which are situated those islands once called Great Britain and Ireland."[25]

The history of the Last Man in English literature followed a very different evolutionary path, beginning in 1816 with a series of poems. The first, and the best known, was Byron's "Darkness," which records the end of humankind, the moon gone, and the world on the point of dissolution:

> The rivers, lakes, and ocean all stood still
> And nothing stirred within their silent depths;
> Ships sailorless lay rotting on the sea,
> And their masts fell down piecemeal; as they dropp'd
> They slept upon the abyss without a surge —
> The waves were dead; the tides were in their grave,
> The moon their mistress had expired before;
> The winds were withered in the stagnant air,
> And the clouds perish'd; Darkness had no need
> Of aid from them — She was the universe. (73–82)

That was the beginning of a vogue for end-of-the-world poems: among others, Thomas Campbell, "The Last Man," 1823; Thomas Hood, "The Last Man," 1826; Edward Wallace, "The Last Man," 1839; and Thomas John Ouseley, "The Last Man," 1853. The theme proved popular enough for the stage. About 1825, Thomas Lovell Beddoes was working on a play, *The Last Man*, which he never

Gustave Doré, *The New Zealander* (1872).

completed. Another in that vein, however, reached the stage in 1833 when *The Last Man; or, The Miser of Eltham Green* by George Dibdin Pitt opened at the Surrey Theater on 22 July. The first half of the century was also the heyday of John Martin, painter of vast canvases that displayed the end of empires and the last days of the human race: *The Fall of Babylon* (1819), *The Destruction of Herculaneum and Pompeii* (1821), *The Great Day of His Wrath* (1851), *The Last Judgement* (1853), and *The Last Man* (1849).

The time was right for a full-length tale of the Last Man, and in January 1826 Mary Shelley published her own account. Shelley's *The Last Man* had a bad reception, with slighting reviews and much ridiculing from furious males. Its critical reputation has improved, however, since the beginning of the post-Hiroshima flood of tales about annihilated cities and the end of all life on earth. At present, there are three editions still in print; and so much has been written in recent years about Mary Shelley, *Frankenstein,* and *The Last Man* that there are not many observations worth adding to the mass of commentaries already to be found. Three brief remarks will suffice. First, Mary Shelley owes nothing to Grainville. He follows the established sequence of events in Revelation to the violent destruction of the world; his Lastness is a program set by God. Shelley ignores all external factors, keeps to this world, and chooses a great natural disaster as death's dark agent. She traces the course of the Plague to the last moment when Lionel Verney, the solitary survivor, sets off on his voyage "around the shores of deserted earth." Second, her story reveals the intimate association between the choice of theme and the mood of the writer. Like Grainville, Mary Shelley had known so much grief that the limitless opportunities of an end-of-humanity story allowed her to shape the world as she pleased. *Requiescant* would have been an apt subtitle for a story in which Percy Shelley is the faultless, amiable, wise Adrian, and Byron is the willful, self-centered, heroic Raymond. Third, the reasons for the lack of interest in Mary Shelley's *The Last Man* when it was first published may be that, as Morton D. Paley suggests, it "was partly be-

John Martin, *The Last Man* (1849). By courtesy of the Board of Trustees of the National Museums and Galleries on Merseyside.

cause its subject-matter was so threatening, and partly because it came not early but relatively late as a presentation of the subject."[26]

Another reason is the slow, erratic development of future fiction before the sudden flood of utopias, imaginary wars, and science fiction stories in the last quarter of the nineteenth century. No more than twenty-two tales of the future appeared in the United Kingdom between the publication of Shelley's *The Last Man* in 1826 and the explosion of future-war stories that followed the appearance of Chesney's warning tale of the German conquest of the United Kingdom in his *Battle of Dorking* in 1871.[27] Most of the pre-*Dorking* tales were one-edition books; none of them started a vogue for future fiction. The take-off only occurred when Chesney's story caused readers to concentrate furiously on the future. *The Battle of Dorking* became the first tale of the future to go into immediate translations — French, German, Dutch, Italian, Portuguese — and into overseas reprints in Canada, New Zealand, and the United States.

Readers in the 1870s looked into the future with the accumulated experience of change that had been growing ever since the appearance of *Memoirs of the Year Two Thousand Five Hundred* in 1772, the first (albeit less than faithful) translation of Mercier's *L'An 2440*. The Franco-German War of 1870 was the first of the modern European wars. Telegraphic communications, breech-loading artillery, railway transportation — these raised serious questions about "the next Great War"; and, in like manner, the crushing German victory changed the relationships of the European nations. From 1871 onward, the tale of the future responded to the many questions about coming things with a great variety of stories: many utopias and some dystopias; marvelous achievements in the air, in space, and in the oceans from Jules Verne; invaders from Mars and atomic warfare from H. G. Wells; and repeated appearances of the Last Man. Richard Jefferies contributed to this new play of as-I-like-it by wiping out the great cities in *After London* (1885) and reducing the European population to the warring tribes of a feudal world. His contemporary W. H. Hudson assuaged his "sense of dissatisfaction with the existing order of things" in *A Crystal Age* (1887), an arcadian vision of small family groups living in total harmony. These were early entries in a growing catalog of tales of the coming cataclysm. In Alfred-Louis-Auguste Franklin's *Les Ruines de Paris* (1875), an archaeological expedition from Nouméa reports on its surprising discoveries in an ancient culture. In John A. Mitchell's *The Last American* (1889), another archaeological expedition — this time from Persia — is a convenient means of satire. Mitchell castigates his countrymen, for the records of the excavators show that the Americans "were a sharp, restless, quick-witted, greedy race, given body and soul to the gathering of riches. Their chiefest passion was to buy and sell."[28]

After the First World, these tales became lamentations for the sudden end of nations or of all humankind. Between the wars, they passed moral judgments on the consequences of bombing planes and poison gas. After Hiroshima and Nagasaki, fantasy had little to contribute to tales of the flash in the sky and the annihilation that would follow. The terror of nuclear warfare found expression in the greatest outpouring of these catastrophic stories in the history of future fiction, as Paul Brians showed in his detailed analysis, *Nuclear Holocausts: Atomic War in Fiction, 1895–1984* (1986). Viewers throughout planet Earth could watch the death of their world on the cinema or television screen in films such as *The Last War* (1961), *The War Game* (1967), *Dr. Strangelove* (1963), *On the Beach* (1959), *The Damned* (1963), and *The Day After* (1983), among many others. There was, however, the beginning of a happy ending to these tales of terror when the Treaty on Non-Conventional Weapons in Europe was agreed to on 19 November 1990. The minute hand on the Doomsday Clock of the *Bulletin of the Atomic Scientists* was moved back by ten minutes, and the tale of the last days of Earth no longer had any power to attract readers. Nowadays, it seems, the Last Man belongs to an almost extinct species.

Book One

CANTO I

Near the ruins of Palmyra there is a solitary cavern, so greatly feared by the Syrians that they have named it the cavern of death. Men have never entered it without suffering immediate punishment for their temerity. The story is told of some reckless Frenchmen who dared to enter this place with weapons in their hands. The next day, at dawn, they were found slaughtered, and their limbs scattered upon the desert. When the nights are quiet, groaning sounds are heard issuing from this cavern, and often tumultuous cries like the shouts of a great multitude are audible. Sometimes the cavern vomits forth eddying flames, the earth trembles, and the ruins of Palmyra move like the waves of the sea.

I had traveled the length of Africa, had reached the shores of the Red Sea, and had traversed Palestine. I know not what secret inspiration guided me. I wished to see that glorious city where Zenobia once ruled and, in particular, that fearsome cavern believed to be the abode of death.[1] I arrived there accompanied by several Syrians. There was nothing alarming in the aspect of the cavern. The ever-open entrance, shaded by the branches of a wild vine, invited the traveler to rest beneath its lofty vault. No monster guarded the entrance; the fearsome reputation of the place alone served to keep it inaccessible.

While I was studying it attentively, I saw above the cavern a man bearing a torch. His eyes were keen and piercing; his majestic brow suggested a profound tranquillity. One would have said that he was at peace with himself, as if he had always lived in that spot untroubled by any knowledge of fear and hope. I know not how he communicated his thoughts to me, but I understood that he was summoning me into the cavern. I felt myself drawn by a sudden and irresistible force; and, in spite of the terror and the cries of the Syrians who tried to hold me back, I leapt into the cavern.

Astounded at my temerity, I walked for a long time in pitch darkness, which increased as I advanced into that terrible place. Suddenly I was unable to move; my feet refused to obey me, and I was held rooted to the spot, motionless like a statue. I could not breathe. I seemed to be in a void where, alive but unable to act, I felt complete repose — a pleasure unknown to human beings, and so delightful as to surpass the most voluptuous sweetness. Suddenly the darkness which shrouded me rolled away, a pure light illuminated the scene, and I saw the objects which surrounded me.

I found myself in an amphitheater built of the hardest stone, facing a throne of sapphire which resembled in appearance the famous tripod of the priestess of Apollo.[2] The throne was canopied in clouds of gold and azure, and held suspended by an invisible power; a still and smokeless flame gleamed from an infinite number of torches. The walls of the amphitheater were covered with enchanted mirrors in which the gaze met an unbounded horizon. To my right, at the foot of an adamantine pillar was chained a powerful old man: his shoulders were bowed, and he gazed with sadness at the fragments of a broken timepiece and two blood-stained wings that lay on the ground.

Then, without using words and by what means I know not, a spirit which dwelt in the tripod addressed me:

"I have punished with death those reckless mortals who, despite the fear which my dwelling inspires, believed that their audacity would gain them entrance. Do not fear a like fate, you whom I have summoned here. I am the Celestial Spirit to whom the entire future is known.[3] All coming things are to me as if they had already happened. Here, time is enchained, and his empire destroyed. I am the father of premonitions and of dreams. I dictate oracles, and I am the inspiration for famous statesmen. As soon as a mortal has committed a crime, I place before his eyes a vision of the punishment that human justice reserves for him; and, in order to make him suffer, I cause him to foresee his own torment and death. If I have guided your steps to this cavern, it is because I wished to lift for you the veil which hides from mortal men the darkness of futurity, and I wish to make you a witness of the scene which will bring the world to a close. In these enchanted mirrors which surround you, the Last Man will appear before your eyes. There, as in a theater, where the actors represent heroes of old, you will hear him speaking with the most illustrious people of the last ages of earth. You will read the innermost thoughts of his heart, and you will be witness to, and judge of, his actions.

Do not think that this is a mere spectacle to satisfy your curiosity. I have a nobler intention. The Last Man will have no descendants who can know and admire him. My desire is that before he is born, he will be known in memory. I wish to celebrate his struggles and his victories over himself — to tell of the pains he will suffer to shorten those of humanity, to end the reign of time, and to hasten the day of eternal recompense that awaits the just. I wish to reveal to the world this history so well worth the telling. However, you must give me your entire attention. This great spectacle will pass rapidly and then will vanish for ever."

After the Celestial Spirit had revealed his intentions, the air rushed back with a roar into the room where I was. I felt it; I breathed it in; it coursed through my veins and restored the movement I had lost. In like manner, everything changed; everything sprang to life around me. The flame of the torches leapt up; the clouds wreathing the throne assumed pleasing shapes; the old man broke his bonds, took up his wings again, and flew away.[4]

Immediately, in the enchanted mirror in front of me, there appeared a magnificent palace, the work of the most powerful rulers on earth, but already showing signs of decay. Beneath one of its colonnades, a woman advanced slowly. From the divine grace and charm of her figure, I could scarcely believe she was mortal, until I perceived from the sadness of her looks that she was unhappy. A young man walked by her side with downcast eyes and, like her, seemed to be deeply unhappy. Then a voice which seemed to come from the tripod addressed me:

"The name of the young man that you see is Omegarus, and Syderia the name of this woman whose beauty has already touched your heart. You are looking on the last inhabitants of earth, those whom your words must celebrate. This undertaking will often oppress your spirit, and, in the belief that the task is beyond you, you will be tempted to abandon it. Do not despair, however, of the power of your guardian spirit. I will sustain your courage. Remember that there are no obstacles that great effort will not overcome."

As soon as the voice had made known to me that in Omegarus and Syderia I was looking at the last precious representatives of the human race, I felt like a traveler who discovers under great tangles of brambles the last vestiges of a famous city. I gazed eagerly on each in turn. When Omegarus claimed my attention, I regretted that I could not give it to Syderia. I wanted to encompass both together in one single look. Already I had begun to love them and was saddened by their unhappiness. Concerned to know the cause, I addressed the Celestial Spirit in these terms:

"I give you thanks for allowing me to witness the last days of the earth, and for choosing me to make Omegarus and Syderia known to the world. To that task I will consecrate the rest of my life. Inspire me with your spirit and your thoughts. Fill my soul with prophetic fire, and lend my voice the proud sound of the trumpet. But what am I saying? Shall I need your help in making men listen when I tell them what fate has in store for the earth and for their descendants? Ah! if the fate of such dear creatures has sometimes troubled their tender hearts — if they have loved the good earth that nourished them — if the hope of living through the lives of their descendants consoled them for their mortality, they will come and ask me for this history. They will spend their days hearing my account, and I shall never tire of repeating my story. Meanwhile, oh! you whom I invoke! Tell me the cause of the unhappiness of Omegarus and Syderia. They are so young to know misfortune! Will misfortune dog the steps of men from age to age even to their last descendants? Will they, like their fathers, water the ground with their tears?"

While I was invoking the heavenly spirit who presides over the future, Omegarus, Syderia, and the palace where they dwelt vanished. In their place I saw an island encircled by a swampy marsh steaming with sulfur and bitumen, and so close to the gates of Hell that the eye could plainly see them from this desolate place. No light from the firmament and the stars penetrated here. The place was lit by the dull glow of the fires smoldering in its depths. Here there was no mantle of green, nor any living creature — even the birds of ill omen and the serpents had fled.

The only inhabitant of this solitary island was a disconsolate old man whose appearance inspired respect and pity. There, in expiation of a sin that he had committed, Heaven had condemned him to watch sinners entering the infernal regions — a torment he had endured since the beginning of the world, and one which had lost none of its power to make him suffer. When he heard the gates of Hell turn on their hinges, his whole body trembled. His white hair stood on end. In great agitation he tried to flee and to turn away his head; but an invisible force held him prisoner. His gaze remained fixed on the trembling victim until the very moment when the demons had thrown the sinner into the devouring flames.

This venerable old man was Adam, the Father of Mankind, banished to this island here by divine justice. It was his disobedience that brought sin into the world. In order to punish him, God decreed that he should be forced to watch the chastisement of his guilty descendants whom he had set on their sinful path. Not knowing how long this torment would endure, he had throughout the ages lived in daily expectation of his deliverance. It never came. He was so worn out with his yearning for deliverance that he no longer had the strength to desire it, and was resigned to eternal suffering. In that moment when hope, dying in his heart, had ceased to soften his pains, he saw in the distance a small cloud advancing toward him more swiftly than the wind. It stopped, and from it stepped the angel Ithuriel — he who, in the garden of Eden, had been the messenger of the Creator.

Greatly moved at this sight, the Father of Men tried to speak, but could only utter inarticulate sounds. His spirit was in turmoil; and the more he strove to control his agitation, the more it increased until it overwhelmed him. At times he seemed to be stupefied — wild-eyed, his whole frame trembling and shuddering — until eventually he regained control of himself. He remained motionless as if resting from a long labor, and, as soon as he could speak, he addressed the angel in these words: "You have the semblance of that celestial spirit who sometimes deigned to visit me in the garden of Eden. How I have suffered since that happy time! Surely eternity has passed since then. Do you come to announce the end of my sufferings?"

And with those words he stopped of a sudden to allow the angel to reply. Open-mouthed, he did not dare to move for fear of missing any of the angel's words. "I come," said the heavenly messenger, "to conduct you to earth where the Almighty has called you to implement the divine plan which He will disclose to you. By supernatural means He will reveal it to you. On the success of your mission depends your deliverance which will come on the very day when the earth is destroyed. I know no more. I can only tell you that a great revolution is preparing. The heavens are in turmoil; the Almighty has awakened from His repose. He has deployed legions of angels throughout the world who only wait for His signal to do His will. At this moment their hosts fill the entire void from the throne of God to the bounds of the universe."

Ithuriel ceased speaking, and Adam waited with eager attention to hear more. Every word the angel spoke filled his soul with hope and joy — he felt himself reborn. "Oh thrice happy day!" he exclaimed, "Blessed is he who comes in the name of the Lord, bearing His divine commands. Can I believe your promises? Will I really behold again the vault of heaven? Will I see again the sun which bathes the world in light, which my eyes have not seen for so many centuries? Will I see once more the lamp of night which was my nuptial torch? I shall see again my children and the soft green of the fields. I shall hear again the sound of human voices."

At these words Adam threw himself at the feet of the angel and clasped them in a long embrace. He could barely support the new influx of feelings until the copious tears of joy began to flow. Finally, he rose and said: "Lead me wherever you wish, if only it is far from this detestable island. Would that I might never return here! I have witnessed passing before my eyes all those guilty souls condemned to eternal suffering, who cursed their first father and the day of their birth. I have seen the gates of Hell opening, a sound which will long reverberate in my ears; and, when they were opened, I have heard the groans and cries that came from that place of torment. At times I have seen the fires of Hell. May those fearful scenes never afflict my eyes again. And now I beg you — you, my liberator — let us leave immediately by the shortest way. Let us take wing through the air."

His prayer was heard. Ithuriel enveloped him in a dark cloud and, without losing an instant, swept him through the skies. They sped rapidly through the airy regions and came to earth in the realms of France, not far from the dwelling place of Omegarus. "Behold," said the angel to the Father of Mankind, "you stand now on the soil where you were first created. If you do not wish to start all over again those centuries of torment on that island you have left, you must bring to a successful conclusion the mission which the Almighty will entrust to you." At these words the angel vanished from his sight, and the cloud which cloaked the Father of Mankind melted away.

As soon as Adam recognized the earth, he threw himself down upon it in a transport of joy. With outstretched arms he embraced it, kissing it fervently. "Oh! my native land," he cried, "my first home, is it really you I touch?" Then, eager to see his surroundings, he rose abruptly and looked with keenest interest around him. The sun had just risen. The Father of Mankind was struck with astonishment when he saw plain and mountain denuded of verdure, lifeless and bare as a rock. The trees were wasting away, their bark encrusted with a whitish deposit. The feeble rays of the sun shed a pale and somber light on the scene. It was not the harshness of winter which had visited this disaster on nature. Even in that cruel season, she would preserve a beauty that spoke of coming fruitfulness. But earth had fallen victim to the common destiny: after struggling for centuries against the onslaught of time, and of men, she was exhausted and bore the sad features of decay. When a son, separated by long absence from a mother whom he left in her youth, returns to find her bowed under the weight of years, he is overwhelmed with grief and embraces her, hiding his tears. Even so, the Father of Men could not contemplate without pain and sadness this decay of nature. "Earth!" he exclaimed, "you whom I saw waking in beauty from the Creator's hands, where are your pleasant hills, your fields bright with flowers, your green bowers? You are a wasteland. Old age has dimmed the light of the sun itself whose brilliance we thought would never die. Now I can gaze upon it without being struck blind." At these words he fell silent as if overwhelmed by powerful thoughts. Then raising his hands to heaven, he cried: "Oh! Thou whose timeless youth outlives the work of Thy hands, Thy glory overpowers me. How insignificant is man, and how great does the Almighty appear amid the fragments of the crumbling world! Thou art the only Being, and I see none but Thee in the universe."

In rendering this homage to the Almighty, Adam was conscious of a great change. A divine flame set his heart on fire; he was moved, transported. It was God who moved in him to enlighten him about the object of his mission. The Deity did not take on any visible form for Adam to see, but instead filled his soul with the light of knowledge, and spoke to him without any need for words. Absorbed in a religious silence, Adam listened reverently to the supreme arbiter of his destiny, and he promised to obey His sovereign commands. He was to undertake a mission to Omegarus. In the name of the Most High — without using any means but eloquence and persuasion — he was to demand from him the most painful sacrifice that the human heart could make.

Adam was filled with fear on hearing the magnitude of his mission; and his anxiety showed in his furrowed brow. "Ah!" he said, "I will again return to the gates of Hell, and there once more begin that cycle of unending torments. Alas! I, whom God created in the sight of the angels, disobeyed the easiest of His commandments, and I am to expect from a weak and imperfect young man the virtue and the strength that I lacked." In great affliction, the Father of Men raised his hands to heaven and prayed to God, who can move the hearts of men when He wishes, that He would incline the heart of Omegarus to obedience.

Then, guided by divine inspiration, Adam went on his way and soon reached the spot where the palace of Omegarus stood. For the Father of Men, the moment was at hand that would raise him to heaven or return him to the gates of Hell. He felt himself so greatly troubled that he could scarcely walk.

And then, Omegarus and Syderia, who had been plunged in a deep melancholy for some days, came out from their home. Troubled that night by sinister omens, they had been unable to sleep: they had seen specters covered in blood walking through the palace with tongues of fire curling round them; and they had heard frightful groans coming from the earth. They were emerging at first light to find reassurance for their troubled minds, seeking in the waking day the peace of mind they needed.

Although Adam, when banished to the gates of Hell, had endured centuries of torment, and although he feared a renewal of his sufferings, at the mere sight of a human being his pains were forgotten. He was going to speak to his descendants, to those children whose first father he was, and to his fellow creatures whom he had not seen alive since he had left earth. What an occasion it would have been for him, if the sweetness of the moment had not been troubled by the cruel task assigned to him. If only he could tell them his name and clasp his children in his arms; if only God had not forbidden him to reveal himself.

Omegarus was astonished at the appearance of this stranger in the solitary place where he dwelt with Syderia, whither travelers had never come. The arrival of this old man seemed a good omen. They thought heaven had sent them a comforter. Their dark fears were dissipated; they regained their lost serenity. Happy the influence of human beings on one another! Two unfortunate creatures meet, and, before they have exchanged a word, they feel already at peace.

Adam was the first to break the silence with the words: "May the peace of God be with you. May He shower blessings on your heads.

May He give you the strength to obey His commandments and the courage to endure misfortune. These are the hopes of an unfortunate old man who holds you dear, whom you would love dearly if you knew his identity."

"Honored stranger," replied Omegarus, "you have already inspired the affection that you seem to desire. Scarcely had we seen you when it seemed to us that heaven had sent us a father. A great joy pierced our sad hearts, for it seemed that happiness had returned."

The Father of Men replied: "Alas! Happiness is rare on earth. It is in heaven that you must seek for it; and that happiness is gained at the cost of cruel pain and much suffering. However, may I ask why you are so sad? Your misfortunes must indeed be dreadful if they come near the grievousness of mine."

"It is only within the last few days," said Omegarus, "that the pattern of our lives has changed. An insuperable fear has taken possession of us. It feeds on everything we do — our work, our pleasures, our conversation, our silence, the approach of night, the return of day, the very precautions we take to banish it. We fear to go on living lest our woes should increase. Fearful portents fill us with terror. Last night specters covered in blood appeared before our eyes; we heard threatening voices; and the palace seemed engulfed in flames. I believe that heaven is angry with us."

"You have guessed aright," said Adam. "You have been guilty of a transgression, and you are tormented by remorse. I know that a great misfortune hangs over you, and I have come to show you how to avoid it. However, you must tell me without any dissembling the story of your woes."

Omegarus answered: "You come at a moment when my troubled heart has need of consolation. Believe me when I tell you that I will open my heart to you. I accept gladly all the help you offer me. I have been guilty of a deed for which I reproach myself. This knowledge is ever present with me. I long for forgiveness, and I believe that my offense is not unpardonable. Hold the torch of truth to my conscience. I am ready to confess my faults. I will tell you, if required, the story of my life, even though I fear your censure."

"If you knew my identity," said Adam, "you would know that I have forfeited the right to pass judgment. Leniency — a virtue of the just — will be forever a duty for me. Open your heart with confidence. I shall be your consoler rather than your judge. If I cannot restore all your former happiness and tranquillity, I can show you how to regain some of the blessings you have lost."

During this exchange, the Father of Mankind had glanced frequently at Syderia. The beauty of her face, her modesty, the fair tresses that fell upon her shoulders, the nobility of her slender and dignified form — these impressions recalled to mind a cherished wife. Eve had, like Syderia, the freshness of the world's springtime and above all the same pleasing modesty she showed when Adam woke and saw her by his side for the first time. When Adam recalled that unforgettable moment, he gave way to tears.

The venerable appearance of the old man, the knowledge of the human heart he seemed to possess, the tears he could not restrain — these won the trust of Omegarus who wanted there and then to tell the tale of his griefs. They were already far from the palace, which was no longer in sight, when they came to a grotto where a solemn silence reigned. It seemed to Omegarus a fitting place for his confession. He seated himself between Syderia and Adam and prepared to reveal the secret history of his life. The tranquillity of the scene was an invitation to listen attentively to the account. The sun was just then rising on the horizon. There was not a cloud in the sky. It was a beautiful day in that dying world.

CAПTO ii

My father was descended from one of the most illustrious houses in the world — one might say the royal family of earth. They occupied every throne in the two hemispheres from such distant ages that history has no record of their ancient genealogy. This palace, the abode of his ancestors, was my father's home. Toward the middle of his reign, he found himself a king without subjects: France, like the rest of Europe, was a vast and empty realm. For twenty years before I was born, marriages had proved sterile. Men, as they grew old, with no children to replace them, thought that the earth was seeing its last inhabitants. My birth was a prodigious event. It caused general astonishment, gave joy to all, and was marked by great celebrations. It is said that women hastened from every corner of Europe to see the man-child, for that is what they called me. My father took me in his arms and, offering me to God, cried out: "Is it really true that this child will be the father of a new race? He is given not just to me but to the whole world. In him alone they hope. Guard him and keep him, for he is Thine. I dedicate my son to Thee."

Their happiness was short-lived. I remained the only child in an aging and infertile Europe. When I lost the parents who had given me life, I had not yet reached the age when men begin to understand themselves. Here, all alone, I performed the funeral rites for my dear ones, and with my own hands I dug the grave where I laid them to rest. These rites accomplished, a great weariness fell upon me, for I found that a magnificent palace, when empty of human beings, is the most melancholy of places. This weariness gradually consumed me, and my youth was wasting away. Tormented by the need for company and the need to express my thoughts and feelings, I resolved to abandon that solitary place. I would go and see if there were any other human beings still alive in Europe.

On the day when I went to my parents' grave to say my last fare-wells, I saw at the foot of a nearby hill a whirlwind of flames and smoke which rose to the summit of the mountain. Although the air was completely still, the billowing flames were driven with great violence toward both east and west, as if they were the sport of con-tending winds. While I was trying to comprehend this phenome-non, the whirlwind raced toward me. I tried to escape, but it pur-sued me, gained on me, and stopped just as it was about to engulf me. I still tremble at the recollection. In the center I saw a man who spewed sheets of flame from his mouth. His body was in constant motion, the locks of his hair waving like flaming serpents. His eyes, blacker than ebony, shone with a gloomy light, and his powerful muscles were like fiery rods of iron in a furnace. This sight, terrible though it was, moved me more to pity than to fear. I was on the point of leaping into the flames to free the unfortunate creature whom I believed to be in pain, when he exclaimed: "Wait, or you will perish without saving me. These flames are my element and sus-tain me. I breathe in these flames as you do in air." That said, he fell silent; and I could see the incandescent flames were drying the tears that rolled from his eyes. As the flames that spouted from his mouth died down, I thought they were about to stop, when he cried out again: "Hear, Omegarus, the dreadful message I have for you. No matter how courageous you are; no matter what dire news you ex-pect, my words will astonish and terrify you even more. This earth which supports you, this earth on which you gaze so confidently, is about to disintegrate beneath your feet. The day of its destruction is at hand."

This news filled me with fear. As a man who has just been told that he stands on the edge of a hidden precipice, trembling for fear of falling, terrified of moving or of standing still, so I feared for my-self. I could have wished to leap the bounds of the universe; I could have wished that a divine hand could carry me to the far corners of the heavens; but I recognized the folly of these vain wishes. I preferred to question the truth of his statement, to refute it in order to reassure my tormented spirit. So, I addressed the strange apparition in these words: "Can it really be that the destruction of the world is approaching so rapidly? There is nothing to presage such an event. The sky is serene. Would not nature feel the approach of the fatal hour and suffer the pains of a last agony?"

"Ah! Would to God that I were mistaken," he replied, "but the awful reality is everywhere apparent. How could I not know the destiny of earth, I the Spirit who presides over its motions? — I who, coeval with the earth, saw it set among the celestial spheres and make its first orbit round the sun; I whom the Almighty called to the summit of the highest mountain in Asia and addressed thus:

'You see these stars which fill the firmament? They are multitudes of worlds, and each of these worlds has its own spirit to watch over it. I have made you the Guardian of Earth. You will have knowledge of the laws that govern it and the elements of which it is composed. It must be your care to prolong its youth and its life. You are destined to live as long as earth endures, and your life span will be not far short of immortality. The lives of many men will pass before you; but, whereas they will wake again to eternal life, your death and the death of the earth will be final. I have decreed in the book of destiny that fateful day when the human race will no longer have the power to reproduce itself.' Thus spoke the Almighty."

The Spirit of Earth continued: "I soon forgot that my life had a fixed term. I outlived an endless succession of generations. The fecundity of the human race seemed inexhaustible, and I believed myself to be immortal. And now, at last, the moment has come when this illusion will be shattered. There is but one woman who, joined with you, can now perpetuate the human race. If you or she should die, the earth will disintegrate, sink back once more into chaos, and my life will be extinguished forever. The danger is now extreme since an infertile race no longer provides an endless supply of victims for Death. His insatiable appetite consumes all living creatures. However, if you are able to escape his clutches to be joined in marriage with the only fertile woman on earth, you will delay the moment of my annihilation. It is not that I place a high value on a few days of life. I know how to die courageously, for I have learnt that hard lesson from men. But I know that the star, which is to rekindle the fires of the dying suns, will soon descend into our sphere to give new warmth and light to our sun. And then, if the earth has escaped destruction, she will wake again to the renewed warmth of the sun. Earth will throw off the garments of old age and put on the brilliant robe of spring. Numerous children will spring from a race rejuvenated, and I shall embark upon a second lease of life. Not merely a few days, but countless ages will be added to my long life. Before I give up this hope, I will summon all the forces at my command — forces as powerful as those of nature herself."

When the Spirit had finished speaking, the fear that gripped me since his revelation of the approach of the last day began to subside. Realizing with some satisfaction that he had a powerful motive to save me, I replied: "If I can advance your cause, then do not hesitate to assign dangerous missions for me to perform. I will not shrink from the task. Young as I am, this heart is not devoid of courage. Many times have I fought fierce beasts maddened by hunger. Alone I have brought them down, and steeped my hands in their blood."

"It is not that kind of courage that is needed now," said the Spirit. "It is the strength of mind that can conceive a grand plan; it is the steadfast patience that nothing can overcome; it is the eagerness that thrives on opposition. Summon up these virtues that distinguish great men. The path lies before you. You are familiar with that city where the English burned the heroine who saved France. Go there and look for a man called Idamas, for it is from him that you will learn how you are destined to regenerate the earth. Do not fear this undertaking. Although I shall remain invisible, I shall be your guide and support." I was about to reply, when he cut me off with these words: "I can stay no longer to hear you. I must return to the center of the earth where I labor constantly to replenish the fires which make the earth fruitful." And with these words he vanished.

In spite of a lingering terror, I was heartened by the pride of knowing that the destinies of earth and of the human race were entrusted to me. So I hastened to carry out the instructions of the Spirit of Earth.

I set out; and I had scarcely traveled westward for four hours, when a great city filled with palaces and ancient buildings met my gaze. The sole inhabitants of this city were a man and his wife whose names were Policletes and Cephisa.[1] They lived by the city gates in a simple and comfortable house which commanded a view of the surrounding countryside. As soon as Cephisa saw me, she called to her husband and exclaimed: "Policletes, there is a man coming to meet us." Policletes showered me with questions. He wanted to know who I was, whence I came, whither I was going, and what was the object of my journey. My youth in particular seemed to astonish him, for he believed himself to be one of the youngest men in Europe.

"My birth," said I, "aroused so much interest that it cannot be unknown to you. I am the man-child whom all Europe came to visit in his cradle." At these words Policletes and Cephisa could not contain their joy. "What!" exclaimed Cephisa. "Are you really the child I saw? Then I was twenty years of age. Those happy times still live in my memory. My mother took me to see the festivities on the occasion of your birth. You were to be, they said, the savior of the world, the father of a new race. The sweet spring was to return once more to make our fields fertile, the summer to give us a golden harvest. It was because he trusted in these promises that Policletes married me. How all those hopes have been dashed! Instead of that regeneration of nature we hoped for, each day brings further decay."

"Be comforted," I replied. "That happy time approaches. It was not predicted in vain." I then told them how the Spirit of Earth had appeared to me. I revealed the commands he had given me, and the burning hope his words had inspired in me. While I was speaking, Policletes could scarcely control his excitement. He was torn between the pleasure of hearing my words and his desire to interrupt me. He wanted to listen and to speak at one and the same moment. Finally, when I had finished my account, he replied: "Let me tell you, dear Omegarus, that your destiny has also been foretold to me, and that already this prophecy concerning you is now beginning to come true.

One day, consumed with anxieties that I wished to keep from my wife, and fearful of that dire future seemingly made inevitable by the continuing decay of earth and the imminence of the last day, I entered a temple close to our home. There God had manifested his powers in marvels which made it renowned throughout the world in days of old. My prayers were so fervent that my imagination carried me away. I felt myself instantly transported to your cradle which was surrounded by a great throng.

There I saw you in all the charms which marked your infancy. As I was gazing on you, your eyes caught mine. You regarded me closely and said with a smile: '*Policletes, your fears will vanish, when you see my wife without knowing who she is.*' I am at a loss to explain the enchanting quality of your smile and of your words, but my apprehensions vanished, and peace returned to my soul. I gave credence to your promises, and my trust has not been misplaced since you are searching for that wife whose presence will end our woes."

As he spoke, Policletes invited me into his house which was nearby, with every show of generous hospitality. I entered the simple dwelling which he had chosen here in preference to the luxurious palaces of the city. His wife hastened to place a meal before me, a meal which surprised me with the abundance and variety of its dishes. I knew not what beneficent deity supplied their wants. I confided my astonishment to Policletes who satisfied my curiosity with these words:

"I have ever been preserved from the horrors of famine. For a long time in the early days, I lived like a savage, constantly moving from place to place. Sometimes I would live by fishing on the banks of lakes or rivers or by the seashore. Sometimes I would find myself in forests, the haunt of wild beasts; and against them I was constantly at war. Tired of this wandering life, I chanced upon this deserted city whose origin, from the evidence of the monuments that enhance it, must be lost in the mists of time. As the solitary lord of this city, I thought that beneath its paving stones there might be fertile soil. Using a lever, I broke up the ground, ploughed it over, and in trepidation planted seed in the furrows. It was successful. If the harvests have not repaid my labors with interest, they have given me enough for my needs. The streets of this city are my gardens and my fields. Indeed, they are so extensive that I shall not soon exhaust them."

I listened with close attention to this fascinating account from Policletes; and I would willingly have stayed to hear more. Policletes and his wife pressed me to stay for a few days, but a task that could not be shirked called me away. I told them that my time was no longer my own: it belonged to the human race. The least delay would be a crime. I assured them that, as soon as my mission was accomplished, I would return to report on its success and to learn from Policletes the art of cultivating the soil. I promised also to bring my wife, who was destined to play so important a part in human affairs. With these words I said my farewells. With tears in their eyes Policletes and Cephisa embraced me. They had seen me as a child, and already loved me as their son. And so I went on my way.

About noon of the second day, I saw a man coming to meet me. He stopped and asked: "Are you the Omegarus who has come in search of Idamas?" "I am indeed," I replied. He embraced me, exclaiming: "I have been guided by Heaven. God has spoken to us. If you only knew what miracles we are promised and what changes are coming. I am Palemos. Follow me. Everything waits on your coming so that Heaven can unleash its power." When he had grown calmer, I begged him to tell me all that had happened. And this was the story told me by Palemos:[2]

"In that city to which we are going there lives a man whose days are passed in studying the historical record. His name is Idamas. His entire conversation is about the nations that once covered the surface of the earth, of their laws and customs, and of the great things that men once achieved by pooling their resources. He relates, as if he had been an eyewitness, the marvelous artistic accomplishments and the deeds of the most illustrious men; and he is filled with regret for the passing of those ancient times which may never be seen again. In a word, his only unhappiness today is the sight of societies that are no more and of the earth a wilderness. Since the sterility of Europe has meant that its citizens were scattered over the face of the earth, his only care year in and year out has been to assemble provisions and gather people round him in order to enjoy the pleasure of speaking with other human beings. This feeble imitation of society is his only consolation.

Yesterday I was among those whom he had called together. I had never heard him speak before. My companions said that the sublimity of his discourse was unequaled and that now he had surpassed himself. Oh! With what eagerness he expressed his desire to see the population revived, society re-created, and the return of springtime to the earth. Entranced in his dreams, he so far forgot himself as to believe the earth was already regenerated. In his fancy he divided the earth among a new race of human beings. He apportioned them empires, instructed the people in all the arts, and taught them the way to wisdom and happiness. He presented these scenes so vividly that we imagined we could see them. Soon, however, on coming to himself, when he compared these magnificent images with the dying world around him, his grief returned, and he could not hold back the tears which flowed freely. We were so profoundly moved that our own eyes filled with tears. Abruptly Idamas rose and left us without a word. We followed him in silence, constrained by an unknown force to follow in his footsteps. He entered the first temple he came to and prostrated himself on the earth, and we did the same. His heart was heavy. We heard his groans. At times it seemed as if he were trying to speak, but grief choked his words. Finally emerging from this agitated state, he rose and addressed the following prayer to heaven: 'Oh God! The time has come to look with compassion on this earth which is dying, sustained by the merest spark of life. Wilt Thou allow the works of Thy hand to perish? If that is Thy design, then spare me the horror of hearing the last sighs of Nature, and grant that before I cross the threshold of this temple, death may strike me down. But if it is Thy will in some future time to change the fate of the earth, I do not ask to see that happy reversal. Merely make it known to us and we will be comforted.'

He had scarcely finished speaking when the temple grew dark and a light brighter than that of day shone round the door of the sanctuary. A voice, which seemed to come from within, resounded throughout the temple. It spoke thus: 'Your prayer is answered, Idamas. Heaven will reward your love for mankind and for the works of creation by making known to you the course of coming things. Joy shall be yours. Earth will be born again, more brilliant than in the days of the first springtime. The destiny of earth is bound up with the life of one man, named Omegarus, who will arrive here tomorrow from the east. You and your companions will conduct him through the skies to distant shores. A book lodged in the sanctuary of this temple will tell you the country where you are to descend, and it will reveal the divine plan to you. But you must not open it until your flight has begun.'

When the voice fell silent, the lights which blazed on the sanctuary doors were extinguished, the temple assumed its normal appearance." And Palemos continued: "Let me describe for you the rapturous joy of Idamas and the transformation these words wrought in him. Gone was the old man bowed under the weight of sorrowful years. Now his bearing had an air of grandeur and majesty, the lines had almost all gone from his brow, and a joyous light shone in his eyes. He had never left our sight, and yet we could scarcely recognize him. He walked rapidly toward the sanctuary. The door opened before him, and there he took the book in which our destinies were written. From there he led us immediately to the place where a number of aerial globes were assembled; and from them he selected a vessel of remarkable size, distinguished by the elegance of its shape and the beauty of the paintings that adorned it.

Then Idamas said: 'My dear companions, I shall not insult you by asking if you are prepared to come with me. Even if you had not heard the commands of God, who among you would refuse the honor of being a minister of His designs in that revolution which will crown your old age and bring about the happiness of future generations? Oh! my friends, what a sublime office is entrusted to us. I vow to dedicate my life to it. I feel once again the burning ardor of my youth. I will lead you in constancy and courage. So shall we see spring bloom once more and nature as beautiful and fecund as our fathers once knew her. God Himself has promised it — you have just heard His voice, and as guarantee you have the young man whose arrival from the east we await. I tell you now, dear companions, that this man Omegarus, who holds the destiny of earth in his hands, is the last son of our royal line. His birth astonished Europe, and it was he whom I saw in his cradle. Know that at that time it was the accepted view of the people that in his reign we would see the regeneration of the earth and of the human race.' Fired by this oration we all swore to follow Idamas, if necessary, to the ends of the earth. Straight away we started on the preparations for our journey. I sought, and was given, permission to come to meet you."

These words concluded the narration of Palemos and gave me renewed hope. For my part, I told him of the orders I had received from the Spirit of Earth. And so, hurrying on our way, we reached the city where Idamas dwelt. We came upon him in the main square, working with his companions on the preparations for my journey. Their wives had gathered there, too, sad and tearful at their departure.

As soon as they saw me, they stopped working and gathered round. Once Idamas had assured himself that I was Omegarus, the last of the royal line and the one he had seen in the cradle, he folded me in his arms, pressed me to his breast, and said: "O my king, can I believe the evidence of my eyes? Can it really be that I hold in my arms the sole hope of the world? I know not into what regions I must take you; but, should it be necessary, I will traverse the entire globe for you. I will open up the barriers that divide the world from one pole to the other. I will set a course through the realms of space and ascend even to the stars. My courage will not fail."

These were his words, and, as if strengthened by my presence, he returned to his labors with renewed vigor.

The capital of Normandy had for a long time been one of the

most famous points of departure for ships of the air. In the many stores of the city, there were still containers filled with those volatile spirits that could carry men above the clouds more powerfully than the sails of ships or the wings of birds. Idamas had already brought these containers to the assembly point. Already the subtle ether was filling out the airship which swayed about, eager for take-off. I looked on with keen interest at a sight which I had never experienced before. The globe especially attracted my attention. On the stern, written in letters of gold, were the words *I have made the journey round the world.*[3]

On the sides there were representations of events, so perfectly executed that the protagonists seemed to live and breathe. Here daring aeronauts sailed over the southern oceans, coming down to land on inaccessible mountain ranges, dropping down to shores the foot of man had never trod, completing the conquest of the world. There, frightful earthquakes, spreading terror all round, reduced cities to rubble. Great abysses yawned wide everywhere to swallow up the inhabitants who were fleeing the troubled earth to take refuge in the tranquil skies. At the center of the globe, fleets of armed vessels darkened the skies. Nothing was more terrible than that sight. The birds had taken flight in terror. The opposing armies, sole masters of their battlefield, advanced on each other armed with glittering scythes poised to cut the cords that held the gondolas suspended, or even more perfidiously they pierced the globe with sharp arrows and small shot. Soldiers fell in thousands as if struck down by lightning. The soft green of the trees grew red with their blood, and their scattered, quivering limbs covered the fields and the roofs of laborers' peaceful cottages.

I had scarcely time to take in these images when I heard Idamas urging his companions to depart. Their wives clung to them, unable to bear the separation, saying to them: "What sorrow we must bear in your absence! We know not what dangers you face, nor whither fate calls you. Even in imagination we cannot follow you to those shores where you will descend. Everything conspires to makes us wretched. If we only knew when our sufferings would end. Alas!

we may be separated forever." At this thought, their tears flowed and sobs stifled their voices.

Moved by the sight of their grief, I wished that I could inspire so tender a feeling in other human hearts. And then I remembered the promises of the Spirit, and my thoughts turned to that unique, incomparable woman whom Heaven had reserved for me. In my eagerness to meet her, I was pleased to see Idamas parting husband from wife, leaping with his companions into the vessel, and giving the signal for the globe to take us up into the sky.

canto iii

Just as a traveler who, advancing across the burning sands of Africa, breathing in the fiery air of the tropics, his mouth parched by searing thirst, upon hearing the murmur of living water, trembles with joy, seeks after the source, swallows the water in great gulps, pours it on his head, his hands, and covers his whole body as if he sought to become one with that element — so the Father of Men drank in the words of Omegarus. He had drawn so close to him that he could follow his movements and gestures. His eyes were fixed on the lips of Omegarus as if he wished to see the shape of the words; his mouth was opened as if to breathe in every syllable. His entire being was listening.

As soon as he heard that Omegarus had traveled through the skies, his astonishment was so great that he could scarcely hide his reactions. Had he not feared to surprise Omegarus by the artlessness of his questions, he would have asked about this marvelous invention. At first he restrained his curiosity, until an overpowering impulse caused him to exclaim, "Oh! Why does the virtue of men fail to match their inventiveness?"

As soon as the words had escaped him, he wished he had not spoken. He regretted the interruption, and, in order to encourage Omegarus to carry on with his story, he fell silent. He listened eagerly, his eyes showing his impatience to know more. Omegarus understood his interest, and resumed the story of his journey.

"Our vessel took off rapidly into the clouds, and there we remained motionless for a time, unable to see the blue of the heavens or the earth we had just left. Already Palemos was reckoning that our inauspicious start was a bad omen, when the dark and gloomy clouds about us vanished of a sudden to reveal the sun once more.

The view revealed was so varied and extensive that we were lost in admiration at the marvelous spectacle. And then the wind started up, filled our sails, and carried our vessel toward the spot where the sun sets over the sea.

The time had come to consult the book of fate. We gathered round Idamas, who took the book reverently, opened it, and read these words: *It is to Brazil and the City of the Sun that I send you.* Thereupon our pilot cried out that the new wind would take us there. Idamas replied: 'Our God continues to protect us.' He then went on with his reading of the sacred book, and we listened in reverent silence.

'Like all created things the earth cannot last for ever. Nature has calculated the instant of its decline, and, like a good mother, she has prepared the means of regeneration. But earth has exceeded the time assigned by nature. Those she has nourished, on whom she has showered her gifts — her own children — will end by destroying her. From her generous hands, they received fruits in abundance, and yet their desires were never satisfied. From her womb, they have hastened to extract the very essence of her life. By taking too much from nature, they have been spendthrifts with their power and have squandered their inheritance. There remains but one remedy for such great evil — the union of Omegarus with the only woman who with him can ensure the continuance of the human race. She lives in Brazil, whither I shall take you on the wings of the winds which are subject to my commands.

As soon as you have arrived in the City of the Sun, gather together all the maidens of that land. You will discover the bride of Omegarus by a prodigy I will perform for her in the presence of the people — a marvel that will make the most skeptical of the Americans believe in you.'

The book contained no other words. Idamas kissed it reverently, and the hope it had given us caused everyone to rejoice. Palemos alone did not join in the general rejoicing. 'Your confidence astounds me,' he said to us. 'No mortal beings have ever found themselves in a situation more perilous than ours. Your own fate and that of all nature depend on the existence of two individuals who could die, and one of them is not known to us. I had hoped that this book, which you look on as a gift from heaven, would at least have guaranteed the success of our enterprise. As it is, we are left in dreadful uncertainty. I even doubt these are the words of the Almighty, for why was He afraid to name Himself? Nothing, my friends, is assured for us, apart from the immense dangers that threaten us.'

This speech terrified my companions. It was then that, for the first time, I had the chance of knowing Idamas. With what vigor did he speak out against the opinions of Palemos. 'You would,' he said, 'require God to guarantee the success of this journey. What right have you to lay down the law to God? Has He ever revealed the entire future to the mortals who have always been dear to Him? Total revelation would have put in jeopardy the truth of His oracles. Men would have refused to accept them simply for the pleasure of accusing heaven of false prophecies. It should be enough for us to know that the Sovereign Master of Nature protects us, and which of us can doubt that? Did you not, Palemos, yourself hear Him tell us His will? Did He not reveal the name of Omegarus before it was known to us? Did He not foretell his departure from the East and the route he had taken in the light of that oracle? Perhaps, to discover the truth of the matter, you rushed to meet him? He arrived, and it was you who presented him to us. And then, consider our vessel which traveled so swiftly and, without the aid of a pilot, took us to those places marked out by destiny. What more convincing evidence do you need to be sure that the Eternal has roused Himself and desires to use us to save the earth and humankind?'

Palemos acknowledged the force of these words. He did not venture a reply and seemed to be ashamed of his mistrust. Idamas, seeing our tranquillity restored, was pleased to tell us about the inhabitants of those regions we could see before us, informing us of their customs and of the most striking events in their history. He showed us in the North the place where England — now swallowed by the ocean — had once been. On the left he showed us ancient Iberia, where Alcmene's son placed the pillars he thought would mark the edge of the world; but he scarcely had time to point out these sights, which appeared and immediately disappeared. Idamas was astonished at the speed of our vessel. Already we were approaching the Fortunate Isles and had begun to make out the Peak of Teneriffe, one of the highest mountains on earth.[1]

These sights moved Idamas. In vain did he try to hide the tears he could not keep back. I asked him the cause of his sadness. 'Ah!' said he, clasping me in his arms, 'these islands remind me of the happiest days of the earth and of its inhabitants. How glorious and virtuous were human beings in those days! How wonderful their deeds! Happy were they who lived in those times. Who would think that we are the descendants of those men, that we inhabit the same earth on which they once lived? How was it that they were privileged to be born in such glorious days? And why are we doomed to live in the last age of the world?' These words of Idamas made me wish to hear about those happy days on earth, and I begged him to tell me the whole story. 'I will do that,' he replied, 'if it is you Heaven has destined to regenerate the world. If you are called to be the father of a new race, you will draw from these accounts the love of good and of the true principles that govern the universal happiness of mankind. We are now starting out over the ocean, where you will find the monotony of the scene dispiriting since you will no longer have anything to see. So, what I have to say will dispel the boredom of our passage.' This was the narration of Idamas:

'For many centuries history presented the deplorable record of human weakness and of the savagery of the passions. It saddens me to tell the painful truth: that experience has been our only teacher. Maxims, more dangerous than the plague, earthquakes, and fire, were for centuries reckoned to be wholesome truths by generations that considered themselves enlightened. It is impossible to describe the damage these maxims caused. They shook all the kingdoms of Europe to their foundations and covered the earth with corpses. Only then did these maxims arouse the horror they deserved. Poisons are only recognized after they have caused death.

The history of such great disasters became a sacred text, which had the effect of promoting wisdom. Every year, a minister gave a reading from the bloody pages of that book, and, on hearing the misfortunes of their forefathers, there was a general revulsion. Some burst into tears; others, terrified by the fearful narrative, ran out of the temple grounds. All of them joined in cursing those damnable maxims which had confused the world and the malign spirits that had promoted them.

Matured by bitter experiences, the human race took giant strides along the road to perfection. Humankind seemed to have reached the highest level of perfection, when a man appeared whose genius made them wonder if he could be a god in human form. His name was Philantor. His predecessors had conquered nature by steadfast dedication to their investigations. Philantor did not need to labor at his discoveries. He had, as if inspired, an intuitive knowledge of nature. All the other philosophers had done no more than raise the veil of nature. Philantor exposed her naked to mortal eyes. The discoveries of the philosophers had often been of no benefit to the world; and sometimes their consequences were m align. Those of Philantor, however, were of positive benefit to the human race. His genius did not decline with his advancing years, but seemed rather to increase. After his hundredth year, he came upon a secret that astonished even him. He discovered how to control the force of fire — to remove and control its heat and, without need to feed it, to preserve it like a fluid in a container. As the master of the most terrible of the elements, he performed prodigies with the help of his obedient flames. He simplified all the sciences, created new ones, and seemed to be God-like in his powers.

An account of just one of his many discoveries — and there are so many that typify his life's work — will give you an idea of this great man. He discovered the secret of prolonging human life and of retarding the onset of old age. In the first flush of joy at this discovery, burning with zealous love for humanity, he exclaimed: 'If ever a mortal desired to be reborn, I have undoubtedly the first claim, since I have reached the end of my days. I am on the point of succumbing to an irresistible force hurrying me toward the grave that waits to receive me. Today, however, I will seal off the tomb. The fire of youth and the heat of the passions will flow again in my veins. Yet I swear to Heaven that it is not my own good fortune that pleases me most. Oh! My brothers, my joy is the greater because of you! Your fathers gave you some years of life, but I will give you immortality.'

Great was his delight as he prepared to reveal his secret. He wished to make the process understood by all, when he was seized by doubts and held back his plans. His fear was that, if he were to give mankind the means of prolonging life, the earth would not be capable of sustaining the huge numbers that would fill the globe. He retreated into solitude; there, cut off from all human contact, he studied and assessed the forces of nature. It is said that, when his work was completed, he prostrated himself before the Creator. He gave thanks that the Almighty had set so brief a span to human life.[2] He acknowledged that the Almighty had set the term of human life in accordance with the size of the earth and the fecundity of its inhabitants; that, if this balance were to be upset, if men prolonged their youth, the earth would not be capable of supporting their too numerous descendants who would fight to the death for living space.

Philantor swore to keep silent about this hidden knowledge that would have such dreadful consequences. He came out of his retreat, pale of face, desolate to see his dearest hopes frustrated. He abandoned his labors, the happiest manifestations of his genius. No longer did he wish to lay aside old age, if he could not share that happiness with his fellow men. Then, desiring only to end his life, he fell into a terminal decline. Lying at death's door, about to breathe his last, he came to think that he saw a way to make his secret knowledge serve mankind. This hope alone restored him to health. Returned from the brink of the grave, Philantor obtained the Fortunate Isles from the monarch who ruled over them. There he caused a temple to be built, girt about with a triple wall fifteen cubits in height and secured with doors of bronze. When this work was completed, Philantor secured his elixir of youth within an urn of gold. He then summoned the ambassadors of all the monarchs to Teneriffe, which he renamed the Isle of Youth.

The name of Philantor was sufficient to cause the kings to dispatch their ambassadors without inquiring about his plans. Their ships covered these waters you see below. The Isle of Youth was scarcely big enough to hold the vast concourse of spectators, gathered from every region on earth. They set up a city of multicolored tents — a splendid sight. When the day arrived for the revelation of Philantor's plan, a round of gunfire from all the vessels gave the signal. The ambassadors assembled and advanced toward the temple to the sound of music, followed by a vast procession of people. That moment will live in history. Philantor, seated on the temple rostrum, the urn beside him, awaited the arrival of the ambassadors. As soon as they had assembled, he appointed a young man with an attractive, sonorous voice to read his statement, which began:

'Hear me, in the name of this venerable old man. When Heaven wished to condemn a man to misfortune, it marked him out for greatness. The wise man, who prefers happiness to glory, refuses to follow the path of greatness and conceals his genius. Society, ever the persecutor of great men in their lifetime, thinks to make up for this mistreatment by elevating them to Olympus after their death — an apotheosis offers an easy recompense. But let us begin by aiming for justice and understanding. Let us not leave it to Heaven to repay the debts of earth. This island, entrusted to me by the kindness of the monarch whose possession it was, I give to the human race. It is a suitable place to bring together the ambassadors of all the kingdoms on earth. And it is here that I call on them to give great men a fitting reward.

Look on this golden urn which contains a mass of flames. The tiniest spark would be enough to rejuvenate the most aged man. Award this prize to that man of genius who is also virtuous. But do not let the sole criterion be a great talent or a singular achievement. Look for a lifetime of dedication — so rare in merit that it could not be replicated. The flames in this container are not inexhaustible. Guard them more jealously than all the riches of the new world. Oh! My friends! You have among you old men, whose reputation both for their work and for their goodness makes a great stir in the world. Make haste to save them from the death awaiting them, for men like these are rarely to be found on earth. In preserving their lives, you are acting in your own best interests. I shall die happy if I can see my contemporaries continue in the land of the living.'

During Philantor's speech, and for a long time after, the throng of people remained like a single motionless body. It was an Indian ambassador who first broke the silence, crying out: 'Yes! There is an old man to whom we must give immortality, if that can be done, and you are that old man. Without leaving this temple, at this very moment, before us all, you must reclaim the vitality of your youth.' A universal cry of assent greeted these words.

In his modest way, Philantor had not foreseen that he would be the first choice of the people. The general acclamation, the outpouring of so many hearts, the arms held out to him — this most touching sight overwhelmed him. 'I am dying,' he said in an almost inaudible voice. At that, his eyes closed, and it seemed that he had breathed his last. There was general alarm. A confused murmur echoed the feelings of sadness and fear throughout the temple. In the midst of this confusion, a young Frenchman forced his way through and rushed to the rostrum. He seized the regenerating flame and applied it to the lips of Philantor. As soon as Philantor felt the benign flame, he moved, opened his eyes to the light, and smiled at the anxious crowd as if to reassure them. Even as they were wondering at this sudden change, an even greater prodigy occurred. Philantor's hair, straggling over his shoulders, grew dark again, the wrinkles vanished from his face, and a manly vigor showed in his person. He stood up, and in his steady, dignified movements, grace and strength came together. He spoke, and the vibrant tones of his voice showed that the full force of human feelings had been restored.

The golden urn was placed in the sanctuary and entrusted to the care of one thousand young men of known probity and courage. Since that time, genius and virtue have received their just rewards on that island. In order to qualify for this reward, it was necessary to have the vote of practically every living person. The test was often too severe and was refused even to the deserving, who expired on the threshold of the temple worn out by long hours of unending toil. The countries that lost them regretted their harshness. These regrets, coming too late, were some recompense to these great men and added to their fame.

Meanwhile, Philantor's initiative had a prodigious effect. One could hardly imagine the works that men undertook to gain such a prize. The monuments raised were so beautiful, so imaginatively conceived, that one can scarcely believe they were the work of human hands. Nothing can compare with the brilliance of their societies, the perfection of the arts, the scale of human virtue. For many centuries, these high standards were universal. Reading the history of those times, it is difficult to believe that such works were those of human beings; it seemed, rather, as if more perfect beings had come to live on earth. In genius and virtue they were giants. When earth had attained so high a degree of glory and of happiness, it began to experience the fate of humankind. Once they had arrived at the perfection of body and soul, the flame began to die within them. Chill old age and death followed. Earth, home to the happiest of mortals — a second Eden — began to lose its fertility. Men, stricken by terror, thought only of saving their environment from imminent ruin. They took their scientific knowledge to the point where they could harness the heat in the atmosphere and concentrate it on frozen lands. They knew how to revitalize the exhausted soil, to make even the dust fertile. This struggle between their skills and the ravages of time and death might well have succeeded in prolonging the life of earth, had it not been for the most terrible event which discouraged them and brought their efforts to nothing.

The sun had just set. A light, brighter than the dawn, blazed in the east and, instead of dimming at the approach of night, it grew stronger and covered the sky in a sheet of flame. Earth reflected the glare of the heavens. The whole of nature — the air and the clouds, the plants, animals and men — seemed to be in flames. Men thought that a new sun had appeared in the sky, or that the day of universal conflagration had come. It was the rising of the moon that had caused this terrifying spectacle. She rose blood-red in the form of a large open mouth spouting torrents of fire. At this sight, the frightened animals howled in terror, and all the people, trembling in anticipation of death, threw themselves face down upon the ground. One wise man alone was brave enough to gaze on those terrible scenes. After contemplating them with a steady eye, he stated that in his view a great volcano was consuming the moon. He observed the conflagration and calculated its duration. Finally, he declared that the sky was again serene. He warned, however, that men would look in vain for the lamp of night — the moon had been destroyed and its ashes, returned to chaos, would help to form a new world.'"

While Omegarus was relaying this historical account given him by Idamas, Adam could not conceal his astonishment. Breaking in abruptly, he exclaimed: "What! The moon is no more! She is lost and my eyes will never see her again!" These words from the Father of Mankind disturbed Omegarus and Syderia, and they looked anxiously at him. They continued to watch him closely. "Do you mean to say," Omegarus asked, "that you have seen the lamp of night? It ceased to exist a long time ago." When he heard these words of Omegarus, Adam leapt up, and, as if the moon were there in the sky, he said: "Oh Lamp of Night! whom I deemed eternal as the heavens, has it been my fate to outlive you and weep over your destruction? How delighted I should have been to see you once more, you who witnessed my happiest hours! How I loved the soft light which illuminated those moments. Seeing you again would have recalled those scenes vividly to mind. Now surely all the important moments in my life have been obliterated."

The First Man, having expressed his grief in these words, remained plunged in a profound reverie; and he only returned to the world around him when his eyes fell on Omegarus and Syderia. The consternation in their faces told him how imprudent he had been. He was filled with self-reproach; and, fearing that he had said too much in his outburst, he made every effort to allay their suspicions. He promised to reveal his identity as soon as he knew their entire history, telling them that they would understand the words he had let slip. Reassured by these promises from Adam, Omegarus took up the story related to him by Idamas.

"'As soon as the earth had lost the moon, her guiding star, the degeneration of our world advanced more rapidly. The resources they had developed to stave off the general decay lost their power. Men were profoundly discouraged on seeing the fields, where they had labored mightily, produce nothing but brambles. Some in fury smashed their tools; others in despair longed for death. Then men began to look on one another as enemies; laws were powerless to prevent murder and banditry. It was even said that many leaders formed an unholy alliance to exterminate a section of the human race. Their weapons were ready, and the night was almost at hand that would cloak the horrible massacre.

That disaster was averted by a minister of religion, born in the French dominions. Heaven had undoubtedly reserved this brave and inventive genius for the last days of earth. When the danger was extreme, he surprised all with resources more than equal to the dangers involved. In the event of failure, there would be no hope remaining for mankind. His proposition was to divert the rivers into new channels and to take over the old courses so that they could be brought under the plough. He told them that they would find virgin land like that cultivated by early men. It was a soil enriched since the creation by the deposits of silt brought down by the waters; and it was so fertile that their harvests would be more bountiful than those the Nile gave to Egypt. He acknowledged that supply would fall short of demand; but he told them that, if they had the courage and patience to undertake these arduous labors, he could promise them that — as Heaven was his witness — he would lead them into a new world greater, more fertile, and richer than it had been in its most splendid days.

The people trusted the words of Ormus. They diverted the Rhône, the Seine, the Danube, the Ganges, the Indus, the Tanais. They caused all these rivers to flow in the channels they had dug, and they cultivated the former riverbeds. Golden harvests returned to delight the eyes of men, and the people blessed Ormus. And so it came about that Ormus, encouraged by such testimonies of public gratitude, dared to propose so bold and ambitious a project that it has never ceased to astonish me. He told them that it was not enough to change the course of the rivers, ponds, and lakes into fruitful fields. Even greater resources were needed. He had promised them a new world, and he would deliver it to them. 'Help me to conquer the ocean,' he said. 'Let us push back the waves, force the waters to retreat into the Southern Continent or our own continent. Let us take possession of the seabed. However, I will not hide from you the extreme peril of this undertaking. If you do not have the skill and the ability to control the wild and angry waves, they will engulf you. But is the terrible prospect of famine a lesser evil than the fury of the sea? I prefer the dangerous course that could lead to our salvation.'

Everyone was appalled at the very idea of this project. Until that moment they had regarded the ocean as sacrosanct. It was forbidden to change the limits set by the Almighty; and if men dared to interfere, they would feel the full force of His anger. It was no easy task for Ormus to inspire them with his own bold spirit. 'How mistaken you are,' he told them, 'in your belief that the Almighty has set fixed boundaries to the ocean. They change every day; natural events rearrange them — an earthquake, a land-slip, torrential rain, an erupting volcano. How often have princes pushed back the bounds of the sea in order to enlarge their own dominions without incurring the wrath of God? Far from fearing His wrath, I believe that He will assist our efforts and that He may have inspired this project to save the human race from ruin. In short, the earth is yours: it is a gift to you from the hand of God. For your needs or for your pleasures, you can level mountains, raise valleys, dig deep into the earth. You have just changed the course of rivers. Drive, if you can, the ocean from its bed. Like the rivers, it is subject to your rule. Build a new world on the ruins of the old.'

And so it was Ormus who proposed the scheme for this famous conquest, and it was Ormus who directed the project. One of his plans was to employ powerful explosives in order to shatter rocks as old as the earth and mountains whose summits pierced the clouds;

and in this way the seas were channeled directly into vast basins. In another of his schemes, he built vast barricades — constructions of genius. They were movable and almost as easy to maneuver as vehicles. When occasion demanded, they could be lowered or raised to a height of one thousand cubits. With the help of these engines, they endeavored to bring the sea under their control. Ormus was as familiar with the world as if it had been his own creation, and he predicted the path the sea would take in its course. At first, he said, like a wild horse, it would resist attempts to master it. With a furious roar it would hurl itself against the barriers in an effort to overturn them. He predicted that, after vain resistance, the sea would retreat before the power of man and pour its raging waters into the channels opened for them. He foretold the route the waters would follow over the continent, filling the gulfs created by the excavations. These would one day be bottomless depths for future navigators.

Ormus had no doubts about the success of his plan. His only fear was that he would be abandoned by men, overcome and disheartened by the never-ending labors required for such a great undertaking. So, he never ceased to exhort and to encourage them. 'I will not speak to you,' he said, 'of the riches hidden beneath the ocean. There in those silent depths, throughout countless centuries, gold and silver, marble and precious stones have been gradually formed. You will find there greater riches and more fertile land than in the beds of rivers where you have toiled. It will be enough for you to sow the seed. Gathering in a bountiful harvest will be all the labor required. What a happy day it will be when, in the place where so many navigators drowned with their treasures you will plant the olive, symbol of happiness and peace, the ever-green orange tree, the scented shrub, and the vine that gives a rich harvest of wine. The first men came into a world covered with trees and flowers. You will have the glory of creating your own world. Your descendants will owe everything to you — the earth they will walk upon, the trees that will shade them, and the works of your hands that will grace it.'

The people took new heart from these words of Ormus. From the coasts of Korea to the shores of Norway there came the sound of tireless hammering. The barriers continued to advance. Ormus asked for no more than five years before they would set foot on the ocean floor.'

Idamas continued with his account, growing more animated:

'Every time I think about this project of Ormus, I am filled with admiration for the boldness of his conception and for the patience of the people who refused to be discouraged by such unending labor. When I walk by the seashore and see the many working areas and the scattered remains of their barriers waiting only for hands to re-assemble them, I cannot hide my sorrow and my eyes fill with tears. Had it been necessary to sacrifice only one man for Ormus to succeed in his enterprise, I would have forthwith offered my life; and I would have renounced all hope of seeing the promised spring and the generations that will descend from Omegarus. What better sight could there be than to see all men united, all shoulder to shoulder in their fight against the intractable ocean? Indeed I believe that Heaven itself would have opened to witness that sublime scene. Whether they emerged from the struggle victorious or defeated, men would have covered themselves in glory.'

Idamas was moved so much that he could barely utter these last words. The faltering voice, the eyes filled with tears, the expression of his face — all proclaimed a troubled soul. He was silent for a while. We shared his emotion and were happy to preserve the silence. Soon, however, impatient to learn what had brought the plan of Ormus to a halt, we begged Idamas to continue with his story. He took it up in these words:

'One day, my dear Omegarus, your descendants may complete this project under more favorable auspices. Difficulties, which human prudence could neither foresee nor surmount, caused the plan to be abandoned. Marriage no longer produced offspring: a large town was lucky to see ten children born in a year. The people then began to murmur against Ormus. They had no posterity, they said. Their descendants would not be numerous enough to be a threat to one another. What need did they have of a new world which they were unable to people? They proposed to give up their futile labors and let Ormus continue, if he wished, with his conquest of the ocean. His sole desire was to glorify his own name. He did not care if they died, ground down by the burden of their labors. He was sacrificing them for his own glory.

Ormus had no need to address their grievances. All work came to a final halt following on an event that no one could have foreseen. Of a sudden, the sun began to show signs of old age: it grew pale, and its rays lost their heat. The northern nations feared for their lives, as their peoples rushed to leave those climes which grew colder day by day. They took all their possessions and fled to the tropics to enjoy the warmth of the sun.

The largest colonies were established in Brazil, while in the north those who survived were hardy and robust men well able to withstand the harshness of the climate. Ormus himself took refuge in the City of the Sun — the destination of our vessel. How thankful I should be if this great man were still alive. What knowledge I should gain from his discourse and what joy I should bring him with the happy news of the coming rebirth of nature. The City of the Sun welcomed him with great joy, and profited from his presence. Winter arrived in Brazil, whitening the plains and freezing the rivers. Then the illustrious Ormus showed men how to melt blocks of ice instantly; and the grateful people proclaimed him worthy to receive the award reserved for genius. But Ormus refused to accept it. He told them that the earth was approaching its final hour; that by prolonging his life, they would make him the unhappy witness of earth's destruction. He begged them to let him die, because he had lived long enough. Nevertheless, he was unable to resist the unanimous wish of the people. I was just leaving childhood behind, when the representatives of all the kings converged on the Isle of Youth, and Ormus had received the last spark from the golden urn. Thus, we had arrived at the end of all things. I know not what has happened to Brazil since that day. But, if it is true that the Brazilian empire possesses the only woman capable of carrying on the human race, then the climate must have undergone a great change and their condition is just as deplorable as ours.'

So ended the account of Idamas, and at this point the pilot interrupted Idamas to say that the wind had dropped. Even the zephyrs held back their gentle breath, and our vessel was not moving. Shrouded in thick mist we had no idea where we were. Palemos thought we were still far from land, hanging over the ocean, and that we must wait for the wind to rise. 'For my part,' said Idamas bravely, 'I dare to assert that Heaven has guided us here and we are above the City of the Sun. I will give the order for our vessel to descend. If I am wrong, we will perish in the ocean, and our fears will die with us.'

The pilot, pale and trembling, obeyed the orders of Idamas. He opened a vent through which the volatile spirits inflating the balloon could escape, and the vessel instantly dropped down to a great square surrounded by magnificent buildings. From the various emblems that adorned them, Palemos realized that we had reached the City of the Sun. I cannot adequately describe our delight. We made the air resound with our cries of joy; but our rejoicing was short-lived, however. We did not know that the cruel laws of that city had condemned all strangers to death."

CANTO iv

"On seeing the French landing, and on hearing our cries which filled the air, the inhabitants of the city came running, weapons in their hands, and surrounded us with menacing looks. Then one of their leaders called Eupolis appeared, and addressed us in these words:

'You are extraordinarily foolhardy to land in a city where all strangers are condemned to death. If you are acquainted with this law, then you know your fate. If you are ignorant of the law, go now. Delay an instant and you will die.'

The people applauded the speech of Eupolis and sought to terrify us with their yells and threatening gestures. Idamas met their fury with calm silence, his eyes downcast. Firm as a rock in the midst of breaking waves he waited until the crowd, worn out by their anger, calmed down. Then, moving toward Eupolis, steadfast in manner, he said to him: 'We are the last descendants of the French nation. The laws of your country are not known to us, for we are separated from you by the ocean. Put us to death, if you wish; but before you kill us, please tell us the reason you have made this barbarous law against your fellow human beings.'

'We did it of necessity,' said Eupolis, his eyes ablaze with anger. 'Bid Heaven give us back our harvests; tell earth not to destroy the seeds we entrust to her. Let our toil and our sweat bring fertility to our fields, and these walls will open to all men whom we shall cherish as brothers.'

'If these are your sentiments,' said the virtuous Idamas, 'withdraw the cruel law you have enacted. The end of your troubles is at hand; the earth will recover its fertility, and many generations will people the land again. All this has God revealed to us. At His com-

mand we have left our country to seek you out in these distant regions, to comfort you with our good news. Would you put your
benefactors to death?'

'Who will assure me,' said Eupolis, 'that you are speaking the
truth? Your speech and your face tell me you are not a villain; but I
fear the credulous man as much as the impostor. By what signs shall
I know that you are not deceived by false hopes?'

Idamas now told of the sudden inspiration which had led him
into a temple in his own country, where God him had given convincing proof of His presence and had revealed His intentions. Idamas
described the form in which the Spirit of Earth had appeared to
me, what he said, and the commands he gave. He then revealed the
intended marriage on which the future of the world depended, and
he introduced me to the people with these words:

'Of all the men scattered across the face of the earth this is the
only one who can perpetuate the human race. Do not be envious,
Brazilians,[1] because he is a European; for one of your number is the
only woman who can bear his child. I know neither her name nor
where she lives. All I know is that she lives in this realm, where it is
my duty to find her.' After that Idamas went on to relate the marvels
of our journey, how God had guided us through the skies, and he
produced the book that the oracle had left with us.

Delighted by this account, the Americans were about to rush
into our arms; but Eupolis, with a single gesture, put a stop to their
expressions of good will. 'If Heaven needs the help of the Americans,' he asked, 'why does it refuse us a sign of its intentions? Why
has God heaped miracles on you, and not accorded us a single one?
Has God exhausted His powers in Europe, or does He think it more
difficult to gain your credence than ours? I will not accuse Heaven
of so gross an error. Indeed, if you want my frank opinion, I do not
think I shall see any more miracles.'

These closing remarks were uttered in tones of irony and insult.
His doubts had humiliated me, and my companions were in despair.
Idamas was the only one to be angered by the obstacles he encoun-
tered. He grew animated in his gestures, his eyes shone with anger,

and his menacing voice could be heard far off, striking fear into all who heard him. First, he questioned Eupolis closely:

'You have chosen a fine time to show such incredible distrust!' he said. 'Our world, one of the greatest works of the Creator, is about to die. If it is God's will to save the world, must He not show His hand and not simply abandon the care of the universe to outdated laws? You wish that He had made known His will to you. What arrogant pretensions! Did you, like us, have to leave your country and cross the ocean? All you had to do was to give us shelter; but then, before granting asylum to others, you demand that God address you.'

Idamas went on speaking to the Americans. He gave them a rapid account of the calamities that were afflicting the earth with ever-increasing rapidity. 'The world and the human race,' he said, 'are on the verge of destruction. At any moment, they can tumble into the abyss and you will do nothing to avert this ruin. So, you will be responsible for the end of earth and of the human race — you will be responsible for your own death and that of future generations. I do not call down on you the punishments of heaven. Indeed, I do not know if Hell has any punishments for crimes of such magnitude. I call Heaven to witness that I have done everything to move you. I shall go now. But no! Let me be the victim of your bloodthirsty laws. I have no desire to live when the hope of happiness is gone.'

Hardly had Idamas ended, when a murmur like the waves of the sea came from the people who had been moved by the vehemence of his speech. Eupolis did not alter his chill attention; and he might have managed to check the favorable attitude of the people, if at that moment a new event had not created a diversion. We heard shouting, cries of joy, all the sounds of people moving rapidly. Soon we saw the inhabitants of nearby areas, drawing wagons laden with birds and the bodies of dead animals. On seeing us, they cried out, 'We bring you an abundance of food.' At this, the populace shouted for joy. They embraced their benefactors, and inquired what deity had given them this great bounty.

The leader of the group who asked for, and obtained, a moment's silence, spoke to us in this fashion. 'Nothing can be more alarming,'

he said, 'than the event to which we owe this abundance that aston-
ishes you. Yesterday, a storm sprang up on our coast, so violent that
its terror is still with us. It seemed as if all the winds had been set
free and had chosen our region for their battleground, all fighting
one with the other. They hastened there from all points of the com-
pass. The first blast was so violent that it knocked down trees with
roots reaching far down in the earth and shook mountains that rest
upon the foundations of the world. At times, the north wind repulsed
the south wind in raging storms; at other times the south wind came
back furiously, driving the north wind like the waves of the sea, taking possession of the air above. Sometimes, all the winds fought together, clashing, turning, diving, vanishing in whirlwinds, swirling
over the peaks of mountains, plunging down with dreadful whist-
ling sounds. The storm abated. A prodigious number of birds darkened the sky; and then came a host of animals who seemed to seek
us out, offering themselves to be killed. We were so shocked that no
one thought to seize on so easy a prey. I was the first to give the signal for slaughter by killing some birds. Thereupon, my companions
followed my example: they felled the animals. And now, loaded with
this abundance, we come to share with you, our brethren of the City
of the Sun, our good fortune which we see as a miracle of divine
benevolence.'

'Truly, it is a miracle,' they all shouted. 'God has declared Himself
in favor of the French. He has performed the miracle that Eupolis
demanded of Him.' In a transport of joy, the people triumphantly
led the way for the French together with the wagons and the inhabitants of the areas close to the palace of Aglauros, the ruler of Brazil.
I walked by the side of Idamas who said to me:

'I expected the success we have enjoyed. May this event be a lesson to us. Perhaps we may meet with reversals, but do not let them
dismay us. God has shown Himself, and He will nevermore abandon us.'

Idamas asked the Americans who accompanied us for news of Ormus. One of them replied that Ormus had made his last farewells
and had left the City of the Sun some three years before. They had

wanted to keep him there, but nothing could change his mind. Neither the sadness of the people, nor the entreaties of Aglauros could hold him back. 'Do not oppose my plan,' he said, 'I foresee that man, driven by hunger, will become the scourge of his fellows. Would you have me wait for the moment when you will struggle with me for a morsel of coarse food, even for life itself? Fellow citizens! While you still love Ormus and retain affectionate memories of him, suffer me to leave you. Why should I to go on living? Why did the people wish to prolong my life? I did not have the will to refuse so cruel a gift; but I am now determined to resist you.' At that, Ormus raised his hands to heaven and prayed for blessings on us. He then departed without waiting for an answer from us, and without even telling us where he had chosen his retreat.

'The departure of Ormus,' the American continued, 'was a general calamity. The City of the Sun was dismayed, thinking that the evils he had predicted would overtake it. It was then that Aglauros banished all strangers on pain of death, in order to manage the resources of his capital and to limit the number of the inhabitants.'

It grieved Idamas to hear of the self-imposed exile of Ormus. While he admired the courageous step he had taken, he pitied him for thinking too readily that Providence had abandoned the human race. He feared that Ormus might have perished in some wild place, the unfortunate victim of his dedication to humankind. Idamas then inquired about the resources of America, the fertility of the soil, the number of inhabitants and flourishing cities. Eupolis, who knew America, answered him:

'Of the many empires that once covered the new world, only Brazil remains. It stretches from the borders of Mexico and includes Peru and the country of the Amazons. The sun in our countries no longer has that heat which, they say, created silver, gold, and diamonds. Temperatures in the torrid zone have dropped and are scarcely at the old level in the more temperate regions. This is no longer that primal land that the savages left to the care of nature. The inhabitants of the ancient world, having exhausted their soil, flooded into America. They cut down forests as old as creation; they cultivated the mountains to their very peaks until they had exhausted the happy fertile land. Then they came down to the shores of ocean where fishing, the last resource of men, promised them an abundant supply of food. From Mexico to Paraguay the shores of the Southern Ocean and the Atlantic were lined with cities inhabited by the last members of the human race. The City of the Sun is the capital of this maritime empire. Built one hundred miles from Cartagena — a long-time rival she destroyed — her port was for ages the meeting point of nations. The City has not lost her splendor. There you will see magnificent paintings, statues so perfect that they seem to breathe, and all types of the most celebrated machines ever invented. Paris, Rome, Thebes, Babylon — they never excelled this city in magnificence. Rich with the treasures of two worlds, she inherits the earth.'

We found that the city was in keeping with the picture Eupolis had given us. It was magnificent, it is true, but it was a city almost without inhabitants, a solitude that filled the heart with sadness and fear. We reminded ourselves that these many handsome edifices had been built as the homes of men. We looked for the inhabitants in vain and were left disconsolate at our failure to find them. In most of the palaces that adorned the city we found rich furnishings and objects in gold and silver, but all that wealth was reckoned to have less value than a tree loaded with fruit or an acre of ground covered with corn.

We arrived at the palace of Aglauros who had been told that his people were bringing strangers to an audience. He was waiting for us, seated on his throne which blazed with gold and sparkling diamonds. Idamas made the same speech to Aglauros that he had previously given to the populace, but he added: 'Great King! at that very moment, when Eupolis and your people were asking for a miracle so that they could believe my words, a great noise was heard. People from the neighboring areas came bringing carts loaded with animals they had killed — animals unknown in this region. At this, the populace cried out that this abundance was a gift from heaven which was favorably disposed to us. We dare to hope, Great King, that you will be of like mind. But if you have any lingering doubts, I will put an end to them when, in your presence and before your people, I will name the wife of Omegarus. God, who sent me, has promised to confirm this in a striking way.'

Aglauros seemed to listen with pleasure to Idamas. That benevolent and amiable prince had only grown cruel and quick to take offence after that moment when earth had refused to feed mankind. The fear that he would soon be unable to satisfy the needs of his people was a constant torture for him. He expected he would one day see them breaking down the doors of his palace to seize the food he had in store. Aglauros seized eagerly on the hope that the French brought him. He repealed the death sentence for foreigners, and he summoned all the maidens in his lands to the City of the Sun. He was most hospitable to my companions, but he ordered that I was to be arrested instantly and confined within the citadel. 'It is with regret,' he told me, 'that I have to be severe with you alone. Idamas promises that miraculous signs will reveal the wife you are seeking in my realm. This last marvel must confirm his august mission and dispel all our doubts. If I were to leave you at liberty, you could choose from the Americans a wife that heaven had not destined for you, and perhaps contrive with her ways of deceiving us. I am anxious that nothing should cloud the triumph of your companions. I want to avert even the suspicion of distrust.' And with that he gave a signal — his guards surrounded me, and I was taken to the citadel.

At the invitation of Aglauros, accompanied by their parents and borne in aerial craft, the maidens of America gathered in the City of the Sun. Some came from the most distant places, from Cape Orange and from Cape Saint Augustine, from the coasts of Mexico and Peru. Idamas, who had made a detailed study of their characteristic types from the history of their nations, told us the origin of these strangers — whether they were descended from Persians or Chinese, Arabs or Egyptians, Spaniards or Romans. He had a sure and felicitous gift for discovering those who were French in origin. These he recognized by their easy manners, their lively and attentive courtesy. He took pleasure in talking with them, in learning their names, the history of their families, and their recollections of their ancient fatherland.

Idamas looked after the strangers like a careful father. He placed them in the finest palaces, and he shared with them the abundance that seemed to increase as numbers grew. He was far from being exhausted by his labors. On the contrary, he derived power and vitality from them. One could say that he had discovered the art of doing the work of several men. He was seen everywhere and he joined in every discussion. The softest melodies did not sound so sweetly to his ears as the hubbub of a vast and many-peopled city. Joy shone in his eyes, and it informed everything he had to say. 'I have seen,' said he, 'the sight dearest to my heart. I have seen the perfect image of the true society. May this coming together of men not be the last.' On another occasion, he exclaimed: 'I no longer fear to die, since I have known the greatest happiness. My friends, let us prolong these happy days. Do not leave me lest our separation prove eternal.'

So, Idamas, abandoning himself to the pleasure he had so ardently desired — to see all human beings reunited in a great society — thought no more of his mission and seemed to have forgotten it. Meanwhile, Eupolis waited in vain for him to name the wife of Omegarus. His mistrust had revived. He was on the point of demanding that the French should fulfill their promise; if he could convict them of deception, he would send them back to their country and demand the head of Idamas. At the same time, the Spirit of Earth, who had the oversight of the world, was no less annoyed by the French, for he was fearful that the loss of a single moment might ruin his plans. He did not, however, suspect the intentions of Idamas, as did Eupolis.

To recall Idamas to his duty, he appeared before him in a dream in that fiery shape he had assumed before me. Anger blazed in his eyes; his voice was terrible and full of menace. He addressed him in these words: 'How secure you must feel! What schemes are you daring to consider in the midst of such fearful dangers? For your sustenance I have caused the swiftest winds and the most powerful means of transport to bring here every kind of creature that lives on earth.

I have emptied the skies and the oceans. The horrors of famine are closing in on you, and all you want is to extend your stay in these parts, and keep a starving people with you.

You know that the Plain of Azas, once famous for its harvests, lies to the east of the City of the Sun. The area can hold a large number of people; when you wake, you will lead the young American maidens there in order to choose the wife of Omegarus. Do this, or you die; and I will entrust the care of my interests to others.' As he uttered these words, the Spirit caused the earth to shake and wake Idamas.

As dawn was beginning to dispel the dark of night, Idamas, thoroughly alarmed, ran to the palace of Aglauros. He was much surprised to find the principal officers of Brazil gathered together in a secret meeting which Eupolis had summoned. Eupolis told them that the orders of Aglauros for the assembling of all the maidens in the land had been accomplished, but in vain, since the French had no intention of fulfilling their promise. It was against Idamas especially that he directed his accusations. 'Yesterday,' he said, 'I surprised him as he was in the act of forming a settlement in this city with the strangers who flock here in large numbers. He flattered them and made much of them, for he knows how to make himself popular. He shows all the signs of an ambitious man. Does he not wish to take control of Brazil with their help? Already he affects supreme authority; for he alone is in command here; and he is the only person to whom the people turn. If you think I am right, we must seize him and interrogate him about his plans.'

At that moment, when the council was about to follow the advice of Eupolis, Idamas appeared before them. As the rising sun dispels by the power of its rays the storm that had gathered in the darkness, so did the presence of Idamas calm the spirits of them all. He told them that he was ready to name the bride of Omegarus, and he asked that the American maidens should be assembled forthwith on the Plain of Azas. His request met with instant approval. The order for action was promulgated immediately, and news soon reached the citadel where I was incarcerated. Do not imagine that I shared in the general rejoicing at my approaching deliverance and at the marriage that would gratify all my wishes. I was enjoying such new and refined pleasures that, fearing to lose them, I received the news with the greatest sadness. My happiness had begun on the day I lost my freedom As the shades of night began to darken the walls of my cell, and as I resigned myself to the gloomy thoughts that the darkness and apprehensions about my future inspired in me, the doors of my prison suddenly opened. I saw a group of young girls enter, their hair loose upon their shoulders, half naked, and many of them with lighted torches in their hands. A woman followed them, clad in a transparent garment silvered like newly formed wisps of cloud in the rays of the sun. Her girdle was the brilliant sash of Iris. In form, she was tall and majestic. Her complexion had the freshness of the lily as it opens in the morning dew. An attractive irregularity gave her features an indescribable charm. An elegant disorder marked her person. Nobility and sincerity showed on her brow.

As I marveled at her in silence, she said to me: 'I am Nature.' At these words, which were undoubtedly a signal, there entered a group of beautiful women who arranged themselves in a semicircle about her. Nature made me sit beside her, and she said to me: 'The women you see here were the jewels of the age in which they lived.' As she spoke, the young girls unrolled a piece of canvas, and prepared a palette and brushes. Then Nature considered each woman, selected the finest features, and began a portrait. 'Look,' she said, showing me a queen in Grecian dress. 'Here is the famous Helen whose beauty was the bane of her country.' On the canvas she sketched the shape of her face, her long flowing locks, and those eyes which lit the flame of love in the hearts of so many kings. From Cleopatra, she took the rosy lips and the arched eyebrows; from Aspasia, her graceful smile; from Laïs, her beautiful hands and shapely arms; from Semiramis, her majestic bearing; from Gabrielle d'Estrées, the happy blending of rose and lily which colored her cheeks.[2] In this way, from these different beauties Nature created one perfect, enchanting woman.

Nature then addressed me: 'This picture, which you think is now complete, seems to combine every charm and attraction. However, it lacks the most desirable of my gifts — divine gracefulness.' And at that, she summoned Eve, and added to her painting that timid embarrassment and touching modesty of the Mother of Humankind, when Adam on waking saw her at his side and gazed enraptured at the beauty of his new wife."

On hearing the name of Eve, the Father of Men broke in on Omegarus, crying out: "What! Have you really seen her?" "Yes," Omegarus answered, "looking young and beautiful as when she first came from the hands of the Creator." This answer increased the perturbation of the Father of Men. Fearing lest his emotion should show, he lowered his eyes, and in this way sought to hide his feelings. He controlled his breathing; his hands steadied his shaking knees. All in vain: he could not sustain the violent struggle. His face grew pale as death. He seemed motionless; his mouth was open, his head bent. He collapsed into the arms of Omegarus and Syderia, who were alarmed because they could not give him immediate assistance.

At that moment, when they feared he would expire, they saw tears glistening in his eyes; the tears grew larger, pouring down his face and restoring him to life. Ashamed of his weakness, Adam moved toward Omegarus, telling him that his last words had reawakened memories that pained him greatly. Nevertheless he had an irresistible desire to know; he asked with timid anxious glances whether the Mother of Men appeared to be happy. Omegarus answered, "In that scene, which passed like a flash of lightning, I had no more than a glimpse of each person. Nature showed me the painting she had completed, and with a smile she said to me that this was the only truly beautiful woman. And then she and her attendants vanished.

The next day, after the tenth hour of night had struck, as I was watching by the dim light of a lamp, my eyes began to grow heavy with sleep. Close to me, I heard the rustling of a dress which roused me. I was astounded. I saw a young woman the very copy of that portrait I had seen the day before. She, however, brought the glow of life to the charms of the painting. Dazzled by so many attractions, unable to restrain my feelings, I started and called out. My reactions, however, had either frightened the fair unknown, or she meant me to show the greatest restraint, for she vanished on the instant. Her sudden departure left me disconsolate. I accused myself of indiscretion, and I was determined, should I be granted the sight of her again, to behave in her presence with all the reverence I would show in a temple at the feet of the Divinity.

The following night, at that same hour, she reappeared in my cell. True to my resolve, still and silent in her presence, I simply gazed at her. In recompense for my discretion, she stayed with me until the dawn and continued to return every night to comfort me in my captivity. Delightful moments! They passed with a rapidity I shall always regret. I fancied I had never lived until then. I felt a new, astonishing life force rising within me. It seemed to me that a flame coursed through my veins, and every day it grew more ardent. If the fair unknown combined in herself the charms of the most beautiful women in the world, it also seemed to me that the passion of all their lovers had passed into my heart. To see her overwhelmed me with delight. I passed the day longing for her return, and the night dreading the moment of her departure.

However, I was not the only one to experience marvelous events. Syderia, brought by her father Forestan to the City of the Sun, found herself in a situation similar to mine. From the moment that Aurora opened the gates of the east until Night who, seated in an ebony carriage, drew a sable veil over the mountains and valleys, a young man, visible to Syderia alone, followed wherever she went.[3] I do not fear, in her presence, to reveal the secrets of her heart. She loved that unknown youth. Her gaze never left him. That pure and solitary pleasure she enjoyed in the midst of her companions, safe from their envious and prying looks. The youth never failed to meet her save on that day when the monarch had summoned the American maidens to the Plain of Azas.

The news of this caused a great stir in the City of the Sun. Everyone said that the end of their calamities was at hand. Shedding tears of joy, friend embraced friend, and even strangers joined in the general rejoicing. The American maidens hastened to adorn themselves. They perfumed their hair; they took out their most splendid dresses;

and round their slender waists they placed girdles of gold. Mothers parted with their most precious jewels to embellish their daughters. Diamonds blazed on their heads, on their arms, and on the fringes of their garments. Syderia alone, sad and unhappy, had no care for her appearance. She wished to stay forgotten and unseen among her companions.

Without losing any time, they moved to the Plain of Azas. So fair a day heaven had not promised for a long time. No cloud veiled the arch of heaven, and never perhaps had any spectacle better deserved the attention of Nature. Aglauros was seated on a magnificent throne. Beside him Idamas placed the American maidens. The French and the kings of Brazil took up the empty space between them and the people. Nothing could be more brilliant than the variety of their charms, or more touching than the attention they inspired. Everyone looked to them as the promise of the longed-for happiness of America.

Idamas advanced toward the people and addressed them in these words: 'This most memorable of days has at last arrived. It will decide if the French are impostors, deluded simpletons, or the saviors of America. For my part, having total confidence in the promises of God, I tell you that He will appear, and He will indicate by certain signs the one among the young women of America who will be the bride of Omegarus. Already I delight in thinking of the advantages that will come from this marriage. I see a new race of men arising to people the earth. The sun will regain its primal heat; the snows that whiten the tops of these mountains will melt in torrents to water your plains; and your fields will see great herds of animals and abundant harvests. The heat will forge diamonds in the depths of Brazil, ripen the grapes on your hills and the golden apples in your gardens. Every kind of rare tree and useful animal which the cold has destroyed will be restored for the benefit of mankind. God will renew the wonders of creation.'

There was a profound silence in the assembly where the appearance of tranquillity hid very different feelings. While a grieving Syderia looked about for the young man who had followed her every day, unable to forgive his absence, the American maidens were eager for the judgment of heaven to be made, but feared that the happy choice would go to a rival. Fathers and mothers shared alike in the hopes and the fears of the daughters. And the people, ever eager to see marvels, were impatient to see the prodigious event Idamas had announced. The French affected a confidence they did not feel. The kings of Brazil watched them closely, still suspicious of the French for fear that they might have been taken in by false promises. Aglauros, however, who feared the ruin of earth might bring on the loss of his empire, gave them his most ardent support. And finally there was Idamas, making his silent prayers to the God who had chosen him to accomplish His plan, begging Him to fulfill His promises.

Followed by the French and the kings of Brazil he approached the American maidens. He looked at them closely, seeking to discover whether heaven had marked their brows with a divine sign. Three times he passed slowly along the line, and three times his expectations were not realized. Already the anxious French wished that the ground would swallow them up; the kings of Brazil were murmuring; and the impatience of the people broke out in uproar. Eupolis said aloud that their error in suffering us to stay had gone on far too long. From the first, he had been right in his judgment of us. They should send us back immediately to our country — the mildest of punishments for our credulity.

Idamas, deep in thought, was deaf to the insults of Eupolis and to the murmuring from the assembly. He seemed as calm as a hermit, lost in meditation by the banks of a stream or in the shady depths of a forest. He was listening to the divine spirit who was speaking to him and enlightening him. He came out of this profound reverie; his eyes bright with joy, he called for silence and spoke to the assembled throng:

'Am I hearing aright? You have ordered your saviors to depart! What reason have you to complain? Perhaps God has not moved quickly enough with His miracles to suit you? You charge Him with dilatoriness — so you want to appoint the time for God to act? You want to instruct Him in what He should do? I could forgive you your impatience, were you not already rich with His blessings. Tell me, you lords of Brazil, did you by your own efforts feed this vast multitude? Did you draw on the fruits of this exhausted and barren soil to bring such abundance within these city walls? What ingratitude! You owe everything to that God whom you revile, who could punish you by leaving you to your fate. Know that heaven, now on the point of declaring itself, requires the presence of Omegarus. Let him come here; and, if you find yourselves deceived, then kill me. My life is forfeit to you.'

Aglauros obeyed the wishes of Idamas. He sent Palemos and several of the Americans to meet me. I waited in fear for the moment that would bring me a wife. Palemos arrived in haste, bathed in sweat, and gave me the orders of Idamas. I set out. As soon as the people set eyes on me, they broke into joyful acclamations which echoed through the surrounding mountains. Soon I was surrounded by the French, and I saw both joy and confidence in the eyes of Idamas. He took me in his arms and presented me to the young American women.

It was not their elegant appearance alone that made so enchanting a spectacle. They were almost without exception beautiful. Their features were finely formed, their complexions whiter than snow, and all were tall and slender like young poplars. But they lacked that inner fire that animates the whole person. Their looks were without vivacity — languid and colorless. Syderia alone had the flame of love which she could not conceal. The deepest crimson colored her cheeks; she made involuntary sighs, her breathing was rapid, and light flashed from under her lowered eyelids. In comparison with her companions, she seemed a heavenly creature, an entirely different being. If a young woman, half naked, were to steal into a sculptor's workshop and place herself upon an empty pedestal — motionless, her eyes downcast — and hope that the spectator would think her one of the surrounding statues, her deception would not impose for a second. Her vitality, which she cannot conceal, would show in her heaving bosom, the coral of her lips, the softness of her breathing. She would stand apart and separate from the cold goddesses that the artist's chisel has shaped. Such was Syderia in the midst of her companions.

The young American maidens eyed me indifferently. I raised scarcely more interest in them than any stranger would arouse. Hardly had Idamas stopped me before Syderia, and she had raised her eyes that modesty kept lowered, when she cried out, staggered, and fell fainting to the ground. As for me, I could not believe the evidence of my senses. I flung myself at her feet, and was so carried away that I have retained no other memory of that moment. In that American maiden, I had recognized the young woman whose portrait Nature had painted; and in me she had found the young man who had followed her every day.

Forestan flew to the assistance of his daughter; and the people, breaking ranks, rushed toward her. Idamas in triumph confirmed that Syderia was the bride we were seeking. 'Have you noticed,' he said, 'that this couple could not look at each other without mutual recognition, without emotion, without instantly embracing? Yes! It is she. I name her, and call heaven and earth to witness.'

Hardly had he spoken, when a new spectacle caught the general attention. In the sky, we saw a garland of vine leaves and ears of wheat which hung for some time in the air, then slowly descended to rest on the head of Syderia. At that very moment, when Syderia opened her eyes to the light, a thousand voices were raised at this marvel to proclaim her the wife of Omegarus. Aglauros and the lords of Brazil joined in this rejoicing; and the French were overjoyed. Eupolis, ashamed of his doubts, embraced Idamas. The American maidens joined in the general happiness, for they had forgotten that they were the rivals of Syderia. For my part, my eyes never left her, and I experienced that supreme happiness that overwhelms the soul. I remained silent, and endeavored to gather all my strength to bear the excess of feeling that weighed me down and exhausted me.

We went back to the City of the Sun, the people singing and dancing for joy. The air rang with repeated cries of *Long Live Omegarus and Syderia!* The Americans and the French crowded round us and gazed at us as if they had never seen us before. Meanwhile Idamas, now more composed, questioned Forestan about his name and origins.

'I am Tupic by origin,' said the father of Syderia, 'the most ancient race of savages in the world.⁴ With their mothers' milk they acquired an abhorrence of civilization. This hatred was made all the greater by an ancient tradition that they held sacred: they believed that the end of the world would come soon after all the Tupics forsook their wandering and savage way of life. In the beginning, they had inhabited the most beautiful regions of Asia. They were driven from there by various peoples who, advancing slowly, pushed them as far as eastern Siberia — a harsh climate, but they preferred it to the loss of their independence. Unknown to them, they had arrived close to a happy fertile land from which they were separated only by a narrow strait. What a memorable day it was when the Tupics crossed that strait and, cursing those who had consigned them to a barren land, came into another Asia, more extensive and fertile than the old one, and above all unknown to the civilized nations! The delights of life in America proved fatal to most of the tribes, and they grew soft. They were the first founders of the empires of Mexico and Peru.

My forefathers, outraged at the sight of the cities they were building, turned away from them and settled in Brazil. There they met new calamities. The Europeans discovered the New World, conquered Peru and Mexico, and even sought to fight with us for the area where we mined the gold and silver they so desired. But their thunder could not subjugate us. They remained for a long time on the coasts we had abandoned to them; but one day our perfidious enemies were able to lull us into a false sense of security. With fire and sword, they took us by surprise when we were weaponless, and they massacred the Tupics. My own ancestors were almost the only ones to escape the conquerors. They hid in the dark forests, in deep caverns, and on inaccessible mountains. Their descendants continued this way of life for so long as the land provided food for gathering and wild beasts to kill for food. It was only when the soil lost its fertility and the forests were cut down that they had to give up their fierce and independent life. Then they were obliged to move toward the rivers and the sea where men, finding there an easy way of feeding themselves, had established their settlements. I, the Chief of the Tupics, have the glory of being the last to leave the primitive state of humanity — the life of the wild. I still have,' said he with pride, 'the quiver and the bow that my ancestors carried and the lion skin that once covered them.'

'I am no longer astonished,' Idamas replied, 'that your family should be the only one that has not lost its primitive vigor. Your forefathers breathed the pure air of the mountains and the forests; they knew the rigor of the seasons and the hard life of the hunter. Rough fare made them hardy; they lived far from the corrupting influence of the town. In short, for longer than the rest of mankind, they remained children of nature. Less fortunate than you, we now are reaping the sad fruits of our fathers' folly. They gave us life when they had exhausted their means of living.'

As he spoke these words, Idamas entered the gates of the city. We were much surprised to find gathered there all the old men who had not been able to follow us. Our songs and acclamations had reached their ears from the Plain of Azas. Impatient to know what event had caused the clamor, they had left their homes and had come slowly to the gates of the city. They wept for joy at the account of our success; they wished to see and touch the crown of vine leaves and of wheat. Some said that they were no longer in fear of death, knowing that they would leave their children happy. Others were envious of those young people who would once more see the sweet spring and fertile autumn. They raised their hands to heaven and gave thanks. And finally Idamas gave orders to prepare my marriage; but it was the wish of Aglauros that a priest should bless our union and that his prayers should draw down the blessings of heaven on Omegarus and Syderia.

CANTO V

"And then Idamas, remembering Ormus, wanted that benefactor of the two worlds to bless my marriage. Those who lived in the City of the Sun had not forgotten his moving farewell address or his genius and his goodness. This priest, beloved of heaven, had on many occasions revealed the future for mankind. He was acquainted with all the ancient prophecies. 'If he approves this marriage,' they said, 'we shall believe that it has received the blessing of God Himself.' They did not know where he might be living nor if he were still alive.

Aglauros had inquiries made among all the visitors who filled the town, asking if any of them knew the retreat Ormus had chosen. Forestan was the only one who could tell us what had happened to that great man. He explained that, when he was bringing Syderia to the City of the Sun, he had passed by the ruins of Cartagena. There, on the shore, he had seen an old man engaged in fishing, but had not been able to speak to him. A man whom he had met nearby, however, assured him that the old man was indeed Ormus.

Forestan was not mistaken. On leaving the City of the Sun, far from looking for one of those pleasant retreats still to be found in America, Ormus had decided to make his abode amidst the ruins of Cartagena, a barren and desolate place. He knew that greedy men would never contest his occupation of this abode since they had abandoned it long ago. Moreover, it was a striking example of the unpredictability of human affairs. This ancient city had witnessed the founding of the City of the Sun. At first Cartagena had despised its nascent strength and then, jealous of its growth, had endeavored to stop it from becoming the reigning power in America; to this end, they had fought a number of bloody wars. After several turns of fortune, Cartagena was taken by storm and given over to the flames. It was left no more than a heap of ruins. There, more than in any other region, the degeneration of the soil was evident. The general barrenness was frightening: a solitary and lamentable place, no growing thing to cheer the eye, no birdsong and no calls of animals, those friends of man who keep him company.

Aglauros instructed Eupolis and some Peruvians to go to Ormus. After a journey of several days, they reached the ruins of Cartagena where a profound silence reigned, as in a town lost in slumber. They made several searches of the place; they shouted out the name of Ormus; and eventually they saw him seated in the vestiges of an amphitheater, shattered columns at his feet and broken statues scattered around. All about and above him there were the enormous remains of ramparts, of temples and of palaces — so vast and forbidding that the eye could scarcely take them all in. On seeing this, Eupolis said to the Peruvians: 'I believe I am looking on a world in ruins.' And then, gazing on the tranquil Ormus who, despite his dreadful surroundings, had found an inner peace of mind, Eupolis added: 'The sage, happy amidst the ruins of the world is no longer a myth.'

Ormus recognized Eupolis and came forward to meet him. He embraced him and asked what had brought him to that desolate spot. 'Honored Ormus,' Eupolis replied, 'I come to gladden your heart by giving you news of a revolution that will change the face of the world. Our troubles are at an end. Marriage will be no longer barren; the earth will recover its fertility — for that we have the assurance of those Frenchmen whom heaven has brought to our land. One of them, a descendant of their kings, has just won the hand of Syderia who, they say, is the only American woman capable of reproducing the human species. Aglauros asks you to bless their marriage, which will be the prelude to happy times. They await only your presence. Deign to follow us and grace the City of the Sun again with the greatest of its citizens.'

As Eupolis continued his address, the serenity vanished from the face of Ormus, and his countenance darkened. Anxious to respond to Eupolis, he seemed scarcely able to hold back the words that rushed to escape from his lips. Finally, he raised his eyes to heaven and, clasping his hands together, he exclaimed: 'What sort of hope do you bring me? How is it possible that you let yourselves be deceived by so grievous an error? Descend to the depths of earth, climb the highest mountains, sound the depths of the oceans, question Nature in every place, and she will tell you that the end of humankind is at hand.' In vain did Eupolis and his companions try to convince Ormus. 'Your coming is confirmation of this dreadful fact. Those ill-fated strangers, foretold long ago, have at last arrived; and now we have the announcement of this marriage which will be the precursor of the last days of earth. Ancient prophecies have foretold that the end of the world will be near when the son of the last king of France comes to marry a young American.[1] In this way, whenever a man wishes to change preordained events, he will in fact be the means of their fulfillment. I shall not refuse to go with you; for you invite me to join in your happiness. I will be with you in your dangers, for I could be mistaken about them. The fearful prophecies which I dread may perhaps relate to more distant times. In the meanwhile, say nothing of my fears. Keep up your spirits. But I shall leave this place with the thought that I may be going to witness the end of the world.'

And then, recovering his usual composure, and as if he had forgotten his fears, he gazed unperturbed on the place he was leaving. 'Here I learnt,' he said, 'that human happiness depends neither on what we have nor on the place where we live. How many delightful hours have I passed here in pondering the wonders of Nature! I find her still beautiful even in her old age. Every day I watch with pleasure as the sun, our luminary, begins and ends its course. I never tire of admiring the many stars that are still perhaps in their first youth while we are about to perish. I recall to mind enchanting scenes on earth, when a thousand different species of flowers were in bloom. It seemed to me that our fathers had often looked on such good things with indifference, and that they were often criminal in the use they made of them. In these reflections I found the patience I needed, and, raising my mind to God, I gave Him thanks for the rigors of my life. Finally,' he added, as he prepared to follow us, 'before I leave this place, let me engrave on these ruins that I lived happily here. But no,' he added gently, 'it would be a fruitless labor. No one will come here to read these words. Happy abode that I have loved, nevermore will you see the face of man, nevermore hear his voice.' With these words, he departed in tears.

In the meantime, the City of the Sun waited impatiently for the arrival of Ormus. And I, in company with Forestan and Syderia, followed the road to Cartagena, willing him to come more quickly. Already the people were murmuring about the delay. Whether Idamas simply wanted to pacify them, or Heaven had sent him inspiration, he then conceived a plan which proved a powerful diversion. 'My friends,' he said to the Americans, 'the day that will see the union of Omegarus and Syderia will remain forever in the memory of mankind. It is not enough to celebrate it with solemn ceremony. Let us begin by inviting the blessing of heaven. Let us raise an altar which will serve as a monument to this august union; and in the fields, open to the face of heaven itself, we should invoke the Divine Presence. More than that, let us invite all nature to these nuptials and, confident in the prophecies that tell us of the world reborn, let us entrust new seeds to the earth.'

Thus he spoke; and so they collected all their implements of husbandry from the places where the rust had long eaten into them. Put to the grinding wheel, they took on once again the brightness of steel. Next, at the head of a long column, Idamas led them to the Plain of Azas, resplendent in the light of the rising sun, and there he drove in the gleaming ploughshare and traced the first furrow. Following his example, all without distinction of age, sex, or rank became laborers again like our first fathers. Some dug into the earth with their spades, turned it over and broke it up. Others with their sharp forks spread manure upon the ground. All found dignity in those labors which, they said, were scorned in the bad old times.

Their labors over, Idamas wished to consecrate them to God so that they would be pleasing to Him. In a nearby temple he had seen an altar where the greatest painter on earth had represented that moment when God had given the powers of fertility to earth. The

Eternal was seated on clouds of gold, bidding all creatures to increase and multiply. At these words a fiery vapor seemed to spring from the sun, and diffuse itself everywhere like the sunlight covering all the earth. The forests spread their branches to receive it, the earth opened up, and the ocean held its waves suspended. All nature breathed it in with delight as though it were a life-giving dew. Already the grass began to appear and the flowers took on the most beautiful shades of alabaster, purple, and the azure of the sky. Already the proud eagle and the fierce lion had shaken off their gloomy lethargy. They seemed animated, and the eyes of all the animals shone with fierce desire.

This altar, which displayed in such vivid colors the marvels we expected, seemed well suited to the ceremony that was in preparation. Soon it was brought to the temple in the Plain of Azas, and, under the protection of that altar, we proposed to sow the seeds most necessary for human survival. Young American maidens carried the seeds in baskets of gold, adorned with rubies and emeralds. Suddenly, an inhabitant of the City of the Sun appeared to announce that Ormus and his deputies were approaching rapidly. We instantly threw down our tools and hastened to meet Ormus. Sounds of joy and of cheerful conversation accompanied our procession. But, as we drew nearer to Ormus, the noise diminished, we slowed our pace, and there was a general silence when the great man appeared before us. On seeing that venerable old man, the glory of the two worlds, who had lived through two lifetimes, each of us imagined we saw him surrounded by the honors he had received in the Fortunate Isles. And when we considered his sublime project of conquering the oceans, we were lost in respect and admiration.

As soon as he learned that we were about to seed the Plain of Azas, he cried out: 'Wait a while! Let us first beg the protection of Heaven. Let me ask God that through me He will bless these seeds which are your only hope.' He then gathered round him the young Americans who carried the seeds; he prostrated himself upon the ground, and lay there for some time in silence. Finally, he mounted the steps of the altar. At that moment he appeared to us like a great and majestic figure, like an angel alighted on the earth. 'Never,' said they, 'has any mortal ever presented a more sublime appearance as God's envoy. What power in his glance! What eloquence in his address! What majesty on his brow!' Then, raising his hands to heaven, Ormus spoke: 'Mighty Creator of the universe, remember the words pronounced by Thee at the beginning of all things, when Thy injunction to the earth was to increase and multiply. Thy creation obeys Thee no longer. Come down from on high; repeat Thy sovereign command; make the earth hear the voice of Her maker. If Thou wilt deign to hear our prayers, we swear here to obey Thy holy commandments, to use Thy gifts for Thy greater glory, to remember forever Thy commands. Each year Thou wilt find us here in this same place, offering on this altar the first fruits of our harvest. We will engrave in marble and bronze the story of our misfortunes and of Thy goodness. We will trumpet abroad Thy praises in a thousand anthems which will be sung throughout the world; and Thou shalt be more honored and better served for Thy regeneration of the world than for its creation.'

After this short prayer he stretched out his hands over the various seeds, and said: 'May Heaven restore your lost vigor; may you be swift to germinate, to raise high your heads, and delight our eyes with the comforting sight of your fruits. And you, Earth, to whom man entrusts his last hopes, receive this precious offering. And so, as a mother on her deathbed hands into the care of a faithful friend her only son lying sick in his cradle, and is unable to suppress her fears, so we are wracked with anxiety. Preserve these seeds from all harm, and in your maternal womb give them warmth, nourishment and life.' So saying, he himself scattered the seeds in the open furrows. His religious faith and eloquent address were an inspiration. It seemed to us that God could not refuse this grace in answer to such a fervent prayer; and we returned to the City of Sun, with the happy hopes of the first tillers of the soil.

A number of days were given over to the preparations for the solemn marriage which was to bring happiness to the earth. During this time, Idamas never left the side of Ormus. He questioned him unceasingly about the arts, sciences, and the most hidden phenomena of nature. Ormus, happy to find in Idamas a learned man, well suited to inherit the sum of human knowledge, lost no time in instructing him. He passed on to him all the discoveries that men had made and bequeathed to him his projects and ideas, as if he knew that his end was approaching.

At last came the day appointed for my marriage for which I had waited so impatiently. It was to be celebrated on the Plain of Azas at the same altar where Ormus had blessed the seeds. All the treasures of the earth, amassed over the centuries, made a rich background to the festivities. Gold and diamonds, abundant in these regions, shone brilliantly on all the vestments. The American maidens sang the loveliest songs ever composed, hymns whose sweet melody ravished the soul and the senses. I walked by the side of Syderia, who will probably reproach me because I praise her so fulsomely; but I must tell you that her beauty outshone all that magnificence. A simple robe of linen, whiter than the lilies of the field, was her only adornment; and her flaxen hair hung loosely over her shoulders. In spite of this sweet disorder, all eyes were fixed on her in admiration, and I had eyes for none but her. I was the happiest of men. Idamas shared my happiness; joy and hope showed on his countenance. Ormus was himself the picture of tranquillity. Whether he had heard from Eupolis under what auspices I had made the journey to America, or whether he was more than equal to any eventuality, that great soul waited calmly.

Things were very different with Eupolis and the Peruvians who had been sent to Cartagena. Ever since they had been told of the oracle that Ormus found so disturbing, their apprehensions had never left them. As soon as they returned to the City of the Sun, they had debated whether to make known the dire prediction confided to them. 'Must we,' Eupolis said to the Peruvians, 'leave the earth and its last inhabitants exposed to the frightful danger they are facing? What if, at that moment when the nuptial torches are lit, we shall hear the sound of the last trumpet? What if we shall see the light-giving sun dissolve, the stars burst into flames, the firmament and the earth collapsing into the void of space? My friends, how we would reproach ourselves for having kept that fateful secret! It is not that I fear death; I have often stared it in the face in the service of this kingdom. However, I confess my weakness. I dread the sight of the earth gaping wide, the confusion of the elements, and the heavens aflame. I fear to live through these terrible scenes. I tremble at the mere thought. My mind is disturbed. I do not know what to think.'

The words of Eupolis touched a chord with the Peruvians who would have taken up his suggestion but for the great respect they had for Ormus. They believed they were brave enough to face a danger which that venerable old man did not seem to fear. They said that they would rather be exposed to every peril than break the promise they had given that great man. Restrained by the decided attitude of his companions, Eupolis did not make public the great secret. He could not help, however, confiding it to the king; he, now knowing the secret, did not attend the marriage ceremony. He gave orders that, if heaven gave the slightest unpropitious sign, the ceremony was to be halted.

Meanwhile, the further we advanced into the Plain of Azas, the more frightened Eupolis and the Peruvians became. They continually shot apprehensive looks at the horizon and the stars. The least breath of air, the tiniest cloud filled them with consternation. Eupolis, in particular, who felt things more keenly, could not hide his alarm. In spite of the prohibition of Ormus, he was on the point of revealing the dreadful prediction and opposing my marriage. But, at that vital moment, he conceived a plan — no doubt inspired by some heavenly being who was watching over me. He left us and made toward the fields we had sown, and with the point of his sword he opened up the ground. It is impossible to describe the scene which met our eyes. Eupolis saw signs of germination! Unable to control his feelings at this sight, he exclaimed: 'My dear companions, our prayers are answered. Nature lives again for us.' Immediately and in great excitement we broke ranks. Each one of us wanted to see the miracle and would trust no eyes but his own. The seed had germinated. Cries of joy echoed from all sides; it was an uncontrollable outpouring of joy. Idamas raised his eyes to Heaven with an expression of profound gratitude, tears rolling down his cheeks. He clasped Eupolis in his arms, because he had been the first to see the bounty of nature, and he indicated that we should carry him in triumph. I shall treasure for ever the memory of that moment. I rejoiced not merely for myself but also for the well-being of the whole community. These feelings were so powerful and so profound that they surpassed even those of love itself. I had almost forgotten Syderia! How agreeable must have been the fellowship of a great people who shared in the same common felicity! Ormus alone looked on these rejoicings with indifference. No doubt he knew that there would be no happy outcome to these first successes.

This occurrence had dispelled the fears of Eupolis and the Peruvians. It seemed that everything conspired to favor my marriage; and, as soon as we were all gathered together once more around the altar, Ormus addressed us in these words: 'It pains me greatly to see your hopes raised. There is nothing more dire than the despair that follows on an excess of joy. I fear that unreliable appearances may have deceived you. The little flames, flickering on the remains of a funeral pyre reduced to ashes, disappear very quickly. Perhaps these seeds will meet a like end. How can we tell if this is not dying nature making a last effort?'

Having roused in us a salutary doubt about the events of that day's proceedings, he continued: 'Almighty Father, if it is true that our labors have Thy blessing, and if this miracle comes from Thine all-powerful hand, deign to hear my humble prayer. Let me live long enough to see the dawn of these happy days and to embrace the heir of the human race. But if our plans do not find favor, do not let them come to fruition. Show us Thy will by some unmistakable sign. I damn to Hell the first person who refuses to obey Your commands.'

At that he turned toward the east, his eyes sweeping the vast horizon. All was calm. It seemed as if nature, desiring our union, strove to smile on us. Reassured by such favorable signs, Ormus approached

Syderia. 'Be you the happy Eve,' he said, 'to this new Adam. I join you in an everlasting union. Look favorably, Heaven, on this marriage. Earth bless this young couple with fruitfulness. May you take their numerous children to your bosom, adorned once more with flowers and fruit. And now, dear Omegarus, with you rest the great monuments of scientific genius — those fruits of enormous labors. You, who will be the lawgiver of the world, endow it with the wisest laws. Remember that cruel institutions oppressed the people for long years before they were abolished. Spare your posterity the return of such barbarities. Let not wisdom be gained at the cost of the happiness and the lives of untold numbers of men. These are my wishes for you and for your children.'

These words of Ormus fired my spirit. I swore in my heart that I would discharge the sacred duties laid on me by so solemn a destiny. I would have been diligent in bringing together the lessons of history and the wisdom of the centuries. Alas! I was about to experience the most terrible catastrophe. The recollection still appalls me.

As Ormus was raising his hands to Heaven in thanksgiving, he paused suddenly. Some object, visible only to him, seemed to claim his attention. He seemed to be listening to a voice which spoke to him, and I could catch only the faintest whisper. He sighed deeply; a frightful pallor spread over his face, and he could scarcely articulate these disjointed words: 'Oh Heaven! . . .What harshness . . . death would be a blessing for me.' Thus he replied to the angel charged with the commands of the Divinity. Later he revealed the message to us: 'You men of Europe have made a great mistake. Heaven condemns this union; and, as far as it is in my power, I now dissolve it. Let Omegarus and Syderia be parted. A curse on Omegarus if he dares to insist on his conjugal rights. Yes,' he said, addressing himself to me, 'you would become the father of an ill-fated race. Your children, driven by cruel famine, would slaughter one another. They would know no god but necessity — the source of all evil. Let Omegarus be torn from Syderia,' he cried more insistently still. 'That is the command of Heaven itself. If you doubt the truth of it, take heed of this portent that will occur before your very eyes. Death awaits me.' With these words, he staggered and fell upon the altar steps.

As he lay dying, another sight no less frightening added to our terror. No one had yearned more ardently for the rejuvenation of the world than Idamas. In pursuit of that goal he had left his native land; he had brought me to Brazil; and he would have circumnavigated the globe. He wanted to think that the earth would once again support flourishing kingdoms. The image of this renascence was ever present in his thoughts, and the force of his imagination had brought it vividly to life. He used to speak to me of the generations to come as if he had already seen them and was already preparing the groundwork for their success. In his greatness of soul, he loved the human race, the arts, the sciences — all those things that could bring men together and increase their well-being. What a blow it was for him to hear the prediction of Ormus and to see his hopes destroyed, to be forced to contemplate again that somber future he believed humankind had escaped. He could not bear this dreadful reversal of his hopes. A burning fever struck him down, and he became distraught. I flew to his side and put my arms around him. I spoke to him, and, although he could neither see nor hear me, he called my name loudly and asked to see Omegarus and Syderia. In his delirium, all the objects of his heart's desire seemed real to him. 'Let them lead me,' he said, 'into the shade of those verdant bowers where I shall find peace in sleep. . . . But what sounds are these echoing through the air? The anvils ring with the repeated blows of the hammers. How I have looked forward to this moment! The arts are alive again in the cities. Look at these ears of golden corn. Hasten, happy laborers, for harvest time has come. How the flowers perfume the air! Let me moisten my parched lips with the fruits of the orchard. Would you abandon me, Omegarus? Where are your children? Bring them to me so that I may embrace them.' He repeated these words endlessly until, completely overcome, he lapsed into unconsciousness and expired.

It was then that Eupolis, terrified at another death, deemed it necessary to reveal the first prophecy of Ormus. 'These events are perhaps the terrible prelude. If you believe I am right, you will lose no time in appeasing the wrath of Heaven which frowns upon this union. We must dissolve absolutely the bonds of this union and send the Europeans back to their own country. Let the ocean separate Omegarus and Syderia. If you refuse to act on this counsel, which God has inspired me to offer, who can tell if this night will be the last for earth? For my part, I am astonished to find myself still alive.'

The Americans were filled with fear. They approved the recommendations of Eupolis, and they demanded that, at dawn the next day, I should depart from their country or be put to death. The barbarians could see in me only a dangerous public enemy. Thus ended that day which began under the most favorable auspices and ended by being the most unhappy day of my life."

Book Two

CANTO VI

Omegarus was about to continue his story when he became aware that Syderia was looking anxious and troubled — he was about to reveal their mutual failings in the presence of a stranger whose censure she feared. Already a modest blush had spread across her face. Moved at the sight of her distress, her husband said gently: "Syderia, my dear, your domestic duties call you now. Prepare refreshments for our guest who has honored us with a visit; and I will come soon to assist you." Reassured by these words, Syderia rose, took her leave of the Father of Men, and departed.[1]

Her departure, however, precipitated in Omegarus a melancholy which he did not reveal. Alarmed by his gloomy forebodings, he followed her with his eyes as if he were seeing her for the last time. His agitation grew greater as soon as she had disappeared. He reproached himself for not calling her back, for it seemed to him that he had just lost her forever. For a long time, he gazed fixedly at the road she had taken, still looking for her until finally he controlled his emotion and went on with the account of his misfortunes.

"I was overwhelmed by these blows of fate, and, stupefied and bereft of feeling, I returned to the City of the Sun without knowing what road I took or what hand guided me. It seemed like a frightful dream which left only the memory of long suffering.

When I emerged from this deathlike trance, the name of Syderia was the first word I spoke. I asked for her; but my companions, forbidden to tell me, dared not reply. I was insistent. My only wish, I told them, was to mingle my tears with hers and to assure myself that our misfortunes had not driven her to despair. It was the only favor I asked, and it was cruelly refused. Palemos told me that the Americans had, under orders from Aglauros, imprisoned my wife far from me within the fortress of the City and in the custody of Eupolis. Hearing this, I realized that she had been torn from me a second time. Despair possessed me to the exclusion of all else. When night had covered the earth in a dark veil, my companions were hastening their preparations for departure by torchlight. I watched their activity with concentrated fury. Irritated by their haste, I said to them: 'Why are you so eager to leave? Here you have nothing to fear. If your concern is to save me from death, you are wasting your time. I swear to you that I will not leave this place where Syderia breathes. Indeed, I will remain here and deliver myself up to the fury of the Americans.'

My resolve alarmed my companions, who strove to dissuade me. They wanted to offer me consolation; but, deaf to their pleas, I challenged them. 'Who are you to offer me consolation?' I said to them bitterly. 'No one is trying to kill you. You are about to return to your own country — the only thing you care about. Everything is in your favor. Is it the business of those who can breathe the freshness of the woodland shade to condole with a wretch on a burning pyre? How could you hope to alleviate my anguish, you who have never known the like? Has heaven not rendered you incapable of feeling it? Oh Syderia! You are the only one in the world who can understand me, the only one whose feeling heart can speak to mine, and they have taken you away from me. They will not even let me say farewell.' Appealing to heaven, I asked 'Why is it not in my power to effect what Eupolis fears? Would that I could see the ocean surge from its bed and the mountains crumble beneath the furious waves, as the earth disintegrates and is scattered through space! Would that I could hear the sound of the last trumpet resounding through the air! Never have I seen a darkness so profound. Would that it were a sign that nature is in mourning in the shadow of death!'

While I was in the middle of my furious outbreak, a man arrived, trembling and pale with worry, whom I recognized as the father of Syderia. 'Europeans!' he said to us in a faltering voice. 'Go with all speed from these inhospitable shores where the inhabitants have sworn to kill you. Take my daughter with you, for it is to her that you owe your lives.' I embraced him and said, 'Yes! Let her come with us; it is indeed she who has saved our lives.' I spoke like a madman, but he had proposed what I most wanted to hear. Palemos asked him for details of the vile plot against us. Forestan told us that, after our departure, Eupolis immediately called an assembly in a temple close by the city and addressed the people in these words: 'Americans! You have just heard the predictions of Ormus. Although they are very grave, an even greater danger threatens you. If the union of Omegarus and Syderia should ever be consummated, it could spell death for you and for the earth. This is the secret that the great Ormus confided to me, which I now divulge in the interest of mankind. Thus, the fate of the world rests today in the hands of one man. Since the rays of the sun first gave light to the world, no mortal man has enjoyed such dangerous power. Do you think it will be enough merely to let the ocean separate Omegarus and his wife? He burns for her with all the fires of love. Nothing has persuaded him to give up Syderia — not the absolute command of Ormus speaking in the name of Heaven, not the fear of the dreadful misfortunes he threatened, not even the sight of that minister of God falling dead at our feet after delivering his prediction. When we were forced to use violence to part them, did you not observe how his face grew deadly pale, how his knees trembled and would not support him, how despair was written in every feature? Such a violent passion is capable of anything. This audacious young man will come back from the ends of the earth, while you are sleeping easily, to reclaim from a fond wife those nuptial rights he has not renounced. He will involve you, your children, and the whole world in universal ruin. Can we live with that continual fear? Heaven has delivered him into our hands. Let us ensure by his death the continued existence of this empire and of the whole world. Let us make our arrangements before tomorrow's dawn. I will go and demand the head of Omegarus from his companions. If they refuse, let us draw our swords and kill them!'

'This counsel was well received. I have to confess, my dear Omegarus, that I too believed your death was necessary. Forgive me for these abominably cruel thoughts. Alas! I was unaware that they were preparing the same fate for my daughter. I was retiring far from her to enjoy a peaceful night's sleep, when I was stopped by a man whom I had never seen before. His bearing was majestic, as if a deity had assumed a mortal form. 'Unhappy father,' he said, 'is your daughter dear to you?' 'By Heaven!' I replied. 'Do you need to ask if I love my daughter? I would give my life for her.' 'Tomorrow,' he replied, sighing deeply, 'she will be in the realm of the dead. The Americans are to engage in battle before dawn. If they are defeated, or if the European escapes them, then they will take the life of your daughter. They believe that the safety of the world requires the death of your son-in-law or of his wife. This course is what has been resolved in secret council with the rulers of Brazil. But I will protect Omegarus. Should the whole of America rise up against him, I will save him. For your part, if you fear for your daughter's life, there is a way to save her. She must leave with her husband. I have redoubled the shades of night which will conceal their flight. But make haste. Every moment is precious.' Forestan continued, 'Come then, my dear Omegarus, I shall restore your wife to you. Let me lose her so that she may live. That is the last wish of a grieving father.'

I was about to follow him, but Palemos held us back. 'I am aware of your grief,' he said to Forestan, 'and while I condemn the cruel timidity of Eupolis, I would rather die than purchase the reprieve of the world with the death of a single one of my fellow creatures. However, I confess, the opposition of Ormus, his menacing predictions, his sad death ever present before my eyes, the death of our leader Idamas — these have filled me with a deep fear that I cannot shake off. Is it for weak human beings to brave the wrath of Heaven, to draw down on themselves calamities likely to appall the most courageous of men?'

'You have nothing to fear,' Forestan replied. 'Hear the words with which the stranger dispelled my fears.' He said that Ormus had lived through twice the allotted span of mortal man. Extreme old age had weakened his reason. He had become fearful and superstitious — in a word, he was no more than the shadow of a great man whose genius had deserted him. He drew my attention to his prophecy that Omegarus would be the father of an ill-fated race, and that the earth would be destroyed on the day of his marriage. One of these oracles was clearly false, and he who uttered them unworthy of my trust.

He pronounced these words with such scorn that I blushed at my own credulity. The stranger took me to the fortress where my daughter was imprisoned. I do not have the temerity to tell you of the marvels by which he demonstrated his power. You would accuse me of lying. But come and see for yourself, and you will no longer fear the threats and predictions of Ormus.'

In the darkness Forestan guided our steps to the walls of the fortress. Imagine our surprise on finding the gates open and the guards asleep. Forestan told us that the stranger had performed all these miracles. We went through the apartment of Eupolis. Sleep had overtaken him where he stood, and he remained standing. I shuddered at the sight of him. From his fierce air and the weapons around him, I concluded that, before sleep overtook him, he had decided on some barbarous course of action. But what horrified me was a glass of poison prepared for Syderia. I would have killed him, had I not been restrained by the thought that it would be unchivalrous to slay a defenseless enemy. Then we entered the prison where Syderia was held. Her father scarcely had time to bid her a sorrowful farewell. He folded her in his arms, bathed her face with his tears, lifted trembling hands to Heaven with a plea to protect his daughter, and gave her into my care in an agony of silent grief.

I know not by what enchantment everything was arranged for our departure, which took place immediately. Our flight was a veritable triumph. Some invisible spirit had already filled our globe with a volatile fluid of a kind unknown to us which filled the air with a most subtle perfume. Our vessel lifted off, carrying us into the air on scented wings. The dark clouds that received us grew bright, giving off more brilliance than the rays of the sun. It seemed that we were borne along on luminous, azure waves; and this miraculous flight lasted until dawn came, and Europe was revealed to our astonished gaze. Such a long journey had been completed in just a few hours.

My companions swore that I was under the protection of a celestial power, and that my union with Syderia had the sanction of Heaven itself. I soon reached this spot, where I tried in vain to detain them; but they were impatient to return to their own country. Everything conspired to hasten that happy moment when Syderia would be mine.

What charm does the presence of an adored wife lend to the dreariest of places! What a change did Syderia effect in that solitude! How beautiful it now seemed to me! No longer did time hang so heavily on my hands day and night. Time had wings again and flew by so rapidly that I would have held him back. What delights filled our days in that short interval of time! Syderia's devotion and care seemed inexhaustible. Each day, I thought I knew all there was to know about her, and each succeeding day I discovered a new perfection. Our souls were as one; my happiness her only joy. She saw that my only happiness was in pleasing her; and the light in her eyes told me that I was successful. Could anything be wanting in such a felicitous state?

The joys of physical union, however, she would not grant me; but I could see in her expression that she refused me unwillingly. When she resisted my advances, she begged forgiveness for her severity by the tenderest attentions and the sweetest and most loving words. This strange combination of love and reserve was incomprehensible to me. Often, after she had long struggled to resist me, her face would be wet with tears. I finally asked why she was behaving so strangely. One day, when she had broken free from my arms, I asked her: 'Why do you repulse me in such a hurtful way? We are as one in everything except this union I so passionately desire. If my eyes show the ardor I feel, you turn from me, and seem not to understand me. You stop me when my words are too passionate. Only if I affect indifference toward you, do you become more affectionate. Then I see the light of love in your eyes; but then, beguiled by this appearance of yielding, if I fall at your feet to claim the reward of my devotion, I encounter coldness again. Oh Syderia! I can no longer endure to live in this way. Tell me, I beg you, why you rebuff me so obstinately. Tell me if I am hateful to you. If so, you have nothing more to fear from your husband.'

Calling on Heaven, she replied: 'Hate you, Omegarus? I who am unhappy only because I love you so dearly. What terrible secret do you ask me to reveal? My tender concern in keeping it from you has spared you the pain that I was happy to suffer for you. But I feel that it would be wrong to remain silent. My struggles have exhausted my courage, and I no longer have the force to resist you unless you are prepared to restrain your ardor.'

When she had finished speaking, she led me to this grotto where you are now sitting, and she opened her heart to me. 'You know,' she went on, 'that after our separation, which Ormus had ordered, Eupolis had me confined to the fortress where I arrived almost on the point of death. Omegarus! I was only anxious on your account. I feared the fury of the Americans who thirsted for your blood. All alone, a prey to the blackest thoughts, I suffered all the torments of anxiety, more distressing than misfortune itself. Then I saw the doors of my prison open as if of their own accord, and my father appeared followed by a stranger. My father, pressing me to his bosom, said: 'You will surely die, unless I restore you to your husband. You may judge the depth of my love for you. I am willing to consent to your departure, to expose myself with the continent of America and the whole human race to all the disasters that Ormus has predicted. However, you can set your father's mind at rest. I know well your virtue. Ormus has broken the bonds of your marriage. Swear to me that you will respect his dying wish.

I took an oath before Heaven, in the presence of my father and of the stranger whom I saw smiling malevolently. He thought, perhaps, that one day I would break my sworn word; but he is mistaken. I shall never be an unnatural daughter. I will never sacrifice a father to my own happiness; I will never sacrifice the earth and its people. If you believe me capable of it, Omegarus, try to know me better.' And with these words she revealed a dagger hidden beneath her robe, saying, 'When my will is so weak and frail that I can no longer resist you, and I am on the point of yielding, I will prevent that crime by killing myself.'

I cannot attempt to describe my surprise and grief. I tried in vain to shake her belief in the words of Ormus and to point out their contradictions and the ambiguities. 'What,' said I, 'has not Heaven attested to their falsity? Have you forgotten the prodigies that made our flight possible; how the plans of our enemies were revealed, their efforts confounded; Eupolis and those who guarded you plunged into a deep sleep?' These arguments could not shake her resolve. She replied: 'I realized that you, being a stranger in America, had no knowledge of Ormus, and that he was revered as a god in these regions. I was brought up to revere that great man, and I believe in his predictions in spite of the ambiguity that surrounds them and in spite of the miraculous events that seem to cast doubt on them. For me, a miracle is less astonishing than a lie on the lips of Ormus. Do not bring new arguments against me. Stop fighting in these battles in which you will only be victorious at the cost of my life. I shall be happy merely to breathe beneath the same sky, to see you, to hear you — this is all I desire. Let me but pass my days in this manner, and I swear before Heaven that I shall have lived the happiest of mortals.'

I made no reply but kept my pain to myself, seeing that it was senseless and dangerous to urge pity for my suffering. I affected indifference toward her. I even denied myself that affectionate companionship which had consoled me for the absence of a greater happiness. I was all the more to be pitied: I burned with a fire made even more consuming by my struggles, and by the continued presence of Syderia who did not hide her love for me now that she had successfully urged restraint on me. Night brought no relief. On my sleepless couch I endured all the torments of an unsatisfied passion. Unable to go on living in this way, I adopted a different course and shunned Syderia, blaming her alone for causing my unhappiness. As soon as daylight came with the dawn, I fled far away from our dwelling and buried myself in the forest. I climbed the highest mountains, only returning when I was exhausted. It was only by such unselfish efforts that I conquered the most unruly of passions. In this manner does the hand that would break a rebellious steed drive him over the furrows traced by the plough. In that effort he wears himself out until the foam from his mouth whitens the bit, the sweat pours down his weakened limbs, and his tempestuous spirit is broken.

To triumph over myself I needed to do no more than persevere in this plan. But Syderia, alarmed by my absences, forestalled my departure one day and said: 'What have I done to you, Omegarus, to make you fly from me all the time? Why do you deprive me of my only happiness? How unjust you are if your aim is to punish me for my resistance. What love and solicitude have I shown you to gain your forgiveness. All in vain! You no longer love me. I have come to believe you might even now hate me.' Having said this, she burst into floods of tears.

Alas! I had not the strength to withstand Syderia's grief. My resolutions were forgotten; I acknowledged the justice of her complaints; and I admitted that I was a wretch unworthy of her tears. I wiped them away, left her no more, and fell back again into the pit from which I had barely escaped.

Such a state of violent emotion could not last. My strength began to fail. I was wasting away day by day, a realization that gave me joy. I delighted in drinking from the eyes of Syderia the poison that was consuming me. To shorten my life, I stayed by her side, finding in this manner of dying a voluptuous pleasure that made vengeance sweet. I told myself that I would die and that Syderia, seeing what she had done, would repent of her cruelty. Her regrets would be in vain, since I would not hear them in the tomb where the dead enjoy the peace that eluded me.

I had touched the end of the scale of violent emotions. Must I tell you to what excess it drove me? I would hide my weaknesses from you, had I not promised to be truthful. I had gone out to hunt and kill the animals that provided us with food. Tired of life, overwhelmed with despondency, careless of the need to preserve a life that had grown hateful, I broke my bow and arrows. After wandering for a long time in paths unknown to me, I entered upon a delightful valley where bounteous nature had brought together all her most beautiful creations. It seemed like Heaven. Each step brought a new transport of delight. The heavenly songs of the birds and the soft murmuring of the streams proclaimed it the abode of voluptuous pleasure. That sensual delight was reflected in several groups of marble statuary where Cupids were embracing half-naked nymphs. Every step was filled with pleasure. As I walked, I scarcely seemed to touch the soft grass. It was a sensuous delight to breathe the perfumed air. An arbor that seemed to serve as a temple was so covered in flowers that no supporting stems were visible. Here I lay down on a grassy bed where sleep — a stranger to me for so long — came to close my heavy lids. What moments then passed! The world of dreams offered me happiness in a thousand different forms: I saw the earth filled with a multitude of people enjoying the blessings of industry and peace, while the fine arts captivated them with refined pleasures. While I was contemplating these wonderful sights, Syderia appeared before me, no longer that stern wife who rejected my love. She invited me into her arms, saying: 'Behold the children whose mother I shall be.' At these words, which filled me with joy, I awoke. No, it was not an empty dream. I saw her by my side with no other mantle but her flowing hair. Amazed and doubting the evidence of my eyes, I touched her. Yes, I felt the beating of her heart and the warmth of her breast. The vision lasted but a moment, and my frustrated desire grew stronger. I swore that she should no longer be my wife in name only. More swiftly than the famished vulture drops from the sky upon the timid dove, I rushed to this spot resolved to make her yield. I no longer feared a refusal, and I was prepared to resist her tears. Alas! I still did not know the extent of her power over me. As soon as I perceived Syderia's room through the evening shadows, my resolve melted away. It seemed as if I were held apart from her, that even over the distance separating us she could impose her will on me. What would have been the effect of her presence, of her prayers, her tender looks, the sacred names of her father and virtue that she would invoke? I felt I would rather die than make an attempt on her virtue. Most of all, I feared that she might carry out her threat to kill herself before my eyes. This image of Syderia, bathed in her own blood, sent a shudder through me. I determined to leave her for ever. 'Farewell, my wife! You are too cruel. I will go far away to end my days. I shall return to that enchanted spot, where I dreamed that you were mine. It was all an illusion, no doubt. But let that illusion return to console me, and I shall not be entirely unhappy.'

Neither the coming of night nor the horror of abandoning Syderia could divert me from my purpose. I convinced myself that I was leaving her for her own good, and thus I excused my crime. I was insane. I abandoned her to despair, alone in this palace. Not knowing where to go, and unable to stay where she was, she was terrified by the darkest forebodings. Finally, convinced that I had been devoured by ferocious beasts, she longed impatiently for the day to come that she might seek my mangled body and give herself up to their rage. What a guilt was mine! But I was no longer a rational creature. Then this delirium which afflicted me began to abate, and I came to myself. I was like a man waking from a terrifying dream where he was suffering in Hell, bewildered, and not knowing whether I was in the land of the living or among the shades of the dead. I hardly recognized myself. I was astonished to find myself alone at night in the open countryside, and I thought that I must be still dreaming. With what dismay did I remember what had happened. I cried out to Heaven. What dismay and fear Syderia must have felt. I flew to her side, fearing I might be too late to save her. She was indeed faint and weak. I concealed nothing from her — confessing my rage, my transports of delight, and my cruel design. Instead of heaping reproaches on my head, she took pity on my weakness, and, taking my hand tenderly in hers, she said, 'My friend, if you do not want to kill me, do not test my courage in such a terrible way. I could not bear it again. You saw how desolate I was and how you could scarcely revive me. May that scene stay in your mind's eye forever; if you should one day form a similar design, may the image of your dying wife hold you back. Would that it were in my power to respond to your desires. I have shed many tears in secret, and if I am unable to hold them back at this moment, it is because of your unhappiness that I weep. It fills me with grief, dear Omegarus, that I must refuse you so cruelly. Let us wait, I beg you, for Heaven to explain its purpose. Do you believe that, if it did not approve my reservations, it would allow the hopes of all humanity to die in us?'

Syderia could scarcely articulate these last words. Her voice died on her lips, she trembled and was overcome. I saw that a most painful struggle was breaking her heart. Exhausted with resisting me, weakened by her heroic efforts, she made to throw herself into my arms. But she then immediately drew back and, to punish herself, she seized the dagger hidden under her robe. I had scarcely time to stop the thrust to her heart. The example of such great courage and my fright at the danger she had run restored my calm. I was ashamed of my own weakness, and swore to behave so as to be worthy of my virtuous wife.

The next days were passed in such tranquillity that I thought I was protected from further storms and that I could think of Syderia and see her without passionate longings and without the struggles to overcome them. My desires were under control. I had not the least idea that I had arrived at the moment that I dared not contemplate — the moment that would crown my happiness.

One morning during my absence, Syderia thought she heard sighing sounds from time to time coming from the subterranean vaults of the palace. Far from being afraid, she felt that tender concern against which the compassionate soul has no defense when it encounters misfortune. She wished to see the unfortunate creature who sighed so piteously. At that moment, the ground shook and a specter enveloped in a shroud rose up. When it uncovered its face, Syderia recognized her father. 'Yes, my child,' he said, 'I am Forestan, to whom you owe your existence. Unable to go on living when you had departed, I descended to the realms of the dead. Restrain your tears. In your own misfortune, it is not for you to weep for the dead. I behold once more the light of day at the command of Heaven.

Hear the will of the Almighty. He condemns the oath I exacted from you. My veneration for the person of Ormus had led me into error; but if my prohibition was wrong, it has served to make your virtue shine forth. I restore to Omegarus his rights as a husband. Rejoice! He will return before the sun has run half its course. If in your modesty you shrink from telling him my commands, go to the temple of this palace, where you will find two pictures over the altar that faces east. Show them to him. On seeing them, he will feel his passion rekindled and your feelings will be made known to him.' Having spoken these words, the ghost of Forestan sank into the ground and vanished from sight.

Syderia remained motionless for some time, and only emerged from her state of stupefaction to search for her father. She wanted to embrace him, to question him, to tell him of her grief at losing him. She lived in hope that he would not deny a beloved daughter so small a favor. She called his name; but whether the dead are bound by rigorous laws, or whether they fear to gratify the curiosity of the living, her wish was not granted. Believing that he had disappeared forever, she wept for him as if he had just died in her arms. Then, curious to see the pictures which she hoped would bring about a consummation she desired, she ran to the temple in the palace. At the sight of the paintings, her surprise was very great, for they seemed to have been only just completed, so brilliant were the colors. The first one represented Eve and her husband in the nuptial bower, where Modesty and Silence guarded the entrance to that secluded spot. A shaft of light, diffused through banks of roses, bathed the scene in a soft, unearthly light. In the middle of this arbor, there was a mossy bed strewn with the petals of flowers. Adam was holding his wife in his arms, beautiful as the eldest daughter of earth must have been. He was leading her toward the marriage bed. One could see on the face of the Mother of Mankind a sweet confusion of emotions — a blushing modesty mingled with the pleasure of yielding to her husband.

The second painting represented their firstborn on his mother's knee. The simplicity of the scene was most charming. Eve, like nature, was in her first springtime. Her appearance combined mature loveliness with the first freshness of youth — an appealing juxtaposition and one never seen on the face of a fifteen-year-old beauty. No picture could perhaps call forth a more tender response; one could not see, without being moved, so young a wife in her role as mother. Enraptured, she gazed on her son whose rosy lips pressed a bosom whiter than the lilies of the field. Nothing could be more gentle than her smile, more affectionate than her gaze. Even her encircling arms spoke of her maternal love."

Hardly had Omegarus ended his description of the paintings when Adam, much affected, interrupted him: "Omegarus, my son — permit me to call you by this tender name. Pause for a moment and let me rest. You have opened in my heart a spring of feeling that I imagined had run dry. Ah! If you did but know who I am. Like Adam, I had a wife and children; and just now I seemed to see and hear them again, to know again the joys of a husband and a father." After that he fell silent, composed himself, trying to prolong the emotions aroused in his heart, but they vanished like the flash of lightning. "Ah!" he said. "How transient are the pleasures of man, impossible to capture and hold in the memory. Continue, my son, with your story. I have regained my composure and am ready to hear the rest if your story."

Omegarus continued. "It was the second picture which most attracted Syderia. The charming sentiment of the portrayal absorbed her completely — it made her long to be a mother, to live again in another, to love and be loved by another. 'What!' she exclaimed. 'Am I to be the mother of a son? In him I would always have the image of his father. Oh! May that happy day come quickly.' Then, seeking to make herself beautiful in my eyes, she put on again the garments she had worn on our wedding day. She surrounded herself with beautiful things, burnt exquisite perfumes, and seated herself on a couch between the two pictures which would suggest what she wished. Ever mindful, however, of the precepts of modesty, she covered with a veil the painting of the nuptial bed.

I arrived. The chamber beautifully adorned, the soft fragrance, the dress worn by Syderia — all filled me with surprise. I drew near to Syderia, and the painting of Eve, her infant son at her breast, caught and delighted my eye, making me wish to see the other painting which was covered with a veil. No emotion could ever compare with my feelings when I saw the Mother of Mankind in her husband's arms. All the fires of love were rekindled in my heart with even greater ardor, for in that wonderful picture I recognized the voluptuous arbor where I had enjoyed such sweet repose and imagined Syderia yielding in my arms. I saw the same profusion of flowers, the same flower-strewn bed, the same softly diffused light. This view awoke new passion in me. The sight of Adam, poised to enjoy all the pleasures of love, emboldened me. Syderia, like the Mother of Men, waited with downcast eyes. A captivating blush rose to her cheeks, and the anticipation of pleasure to come made her heart beat faster. Without enquiring to what heavenly power I was indebted for this change, I made Syderia my wife. The earth trembled with joy. Soft murmurs and melodious sounds filled the air. But, at the same moment, the sun grew dark, images of blood reddened the skies, and I have often since seen the same phenomena. The timid Syderia was terrified. While I sought to reassure and console her, I myself was filled with remorse as if I had committed a crime. And yet would the Almighty permit the dead to rise from their graves in order to deceive men? It was Forestan who spoke, and he was no illusion. Who but he could have placed those paintings of the earthly paradise upon the altar? Who other than he would have revealed them to Syderia? There has been no other portent to announce the end of the world as foretold by Ormus. The sky is serene; the sun has not changed its course. And since that day, the earth has continued to present a smiling face and seems to have grown young again. Why, then, am I unable to escape from feelings of melancholy and fear? Oh you, whom Heaven has brought here, tell me why. Give me back my peace of mind! Or, if I cannot hope for that, tell me the truth. I have hidden nothing from you, and I do not fear to hear the truth."

CANTO VII

As soon as Omegarus had finished speaking, all the watching powers of Heaven fixed their gaze on the First Man. They knew not the object of his mission; they knew only that the most terrible events since the creation of the world were about to happen. Adam lifted his hands to Heaven, calling on the Almighty to inspire him and to give him the strength and the counsel he needed. As soon as he had finished these prayers, he found himself caught up in swirling rays of light. God Himself appeared before him, unchanged since those first days of creation when He revealed himself to Adam in the Garden of Eden. Adam recognized his Creator, and with joyful heart he knelt in adoration. But the commands he received filled him with sorrow. He rose hastily, fear on his countenance, his entire body trembling. He seized the hand of Omegarus, and dragged him away far from his palace, as if the spot were blighted by a fatal contagion.[1]

In vain did Omegarus try to hold back, reminding him that Syderia was waiting for them. Adam, his voice trembling with fear, replied: "You must follow me, or the most terrible calamities will befall you." The two of them walked in silence in the direction of that famous city, once the capital of the French Empire. Omegarus did not dare to question the Father of Men, and Adam shrank from carrying out the mission with which God had charged him. When they had made a good two hours' march from Syderia, they stopped on a hillside. From there, they could make out the winding course of the Seine, which men had now diverted.

The Father of Men embraced Omegarus and gave way to the tears he could no longer hold back. In a faltering voice, he said: "How is it that sorrow has not exhausted my store of tears, I who since the death of Adam have marked every moment by counting them? Could

I have ever thought that my misfortunes would grow greater? Ah! Why am I not still before the gates of Hell? I now miss even that horrible abode. I love you, Omegarus, as the dearest of my children. Your sufferings fill to overflowing the measure of mine. I have just parted you from Syderia forever. God ordains that you leave her."

"Does Heaven wish her to die?" Omegarus replied sharply. "It could be," Adam answered, "that God, who speaks to you through my mouth, He whose will decides the destiny of mankind, ordains her death."

At this reply from Adam, Omegarus reeled and grew pale. He tried to speak but no sound came from his lips. Adam allowed this dreadful moment to pass in silence. He knew there were no words to alleviate such cruel suffering. In a despairing tone, Omegarus asked: "What crime has Syderia committed that she should be condemned to death? Could it be possible that Heaven condemns our marriage? Can it be true that an accursed race will spring from it? Are the predictions of Ormus to be realized?" Adam replied: "Unhappy man! Syderia carries in her womb the child who is destined to be the father of a frightful progeny — a child that should never have been conceived."

At this news Omegarus gave way to violent and conflicting emotions. As the waves of the sea, tempest-tossed, rise mountain-high and suddenly fall back into the deepest troughs, so Omegarus went from one extreme to another. At one time he would make the boldest resolutions, brave every danger, defy the wrath of Heaven and endure all the woes that were to be his lot. At other times, weighed down by the weight of his troubles, he was as feeble as a child, and ready to give way to tears. Finally, blushing at his own weakness, he summoned all his courage and resolved to resist the Father of Men. In a firm voice, he replied, "The child, of which I am the father, far from breaking the bonds that unite me to Syderia, will further strengthen them. The child is a gift from Heaven, a pledge of its favor, and I shall guard and keep it. I would not have known the joys of love, had not Syderia longed for a child of mine who would have beguiled the solitary hours of her existence. And now when I learn that her prayers are answered, you choose that very moment to decree a barbarous separation. I will never agree to it! I will listen to you no longer; and I will fly to forget your commands in the arms of Syderia."

But the Father of Men immediately cried out, "Do not go! What kind of foolhardy act do you have in mind? Hear now the disasters that I was anxious to hide from you, but which you now force me to reveal. Learn that this child will raise a murderous hand against his mother and father, and that this atrocious crime will be the least of his evil deeds."

Omegarus grew more and more angry with this stranger whose every word was a dagger in his heart. He gave him wrathful looks and his anger blazed out in these words: "Take your lying oracles elsewhere; they cannot frighten me. By what authority do you try to convince me? Perhaps you think that you have already succeeded. You are mistaken. I still do not know who you are because, like all impostors, you have concealed from me your name and your country. It is true that you claim to be an envoy of Heaven, but did you think that your word alone would be enough for me? Ranged against you are all the inconsistencies that devalued the prophecies of Ormus, the oracles granted to Idamas, as well as the numerous miracles I have witnessed and the testimony of Forestan returned from the realm of the dead. When you shall have performed wonders as great as these, when temples deliver oracles in your presence, when the dead rise from their graves and confirm your words, then your threats might frighten me and perhaps make me consider obeying your commands."

The Father of Men had anticipated this furious outburst from Omegarus. In his own mind, he excused him and did not think his reproaches excessive. He answered in these words: "A man who thinks like Ormus has no need to perform miracles; and you would believe my words if they coincided with the wishes of your own heart. With a single word I shall shake your confidence. The oracles delivered in the presence of Ormus, the prodigies you have witnessed, the apparition of Forestan — all of which have reassured you — were illusions, the work of the Spirit of Earth. It was he who, concealed in a sanctuary, dared to imitate the voice of God and played on the inclinations of the gullible Idamas. He was the one who, when you were in prison, conjured up the spectacle of the most beautiful women in the world and brought before you the vision of Syderia. He it was who made the Plain of Azas appear fruitful before the amazed eyes of the Brazilians; and he who, assuming the voice and features of Forestan, appeared to his daughter in order to ensure that she yielded to your desires. How could you have failed to see through his deception? He must die if you do not give the world a new posterity. It was easy to foresee that he would employ all his secret knowledge and his power to bring about a marriage that would be his salvation.

You have been deceived in all things, except in the predictions that Heaven made to console Polycletes, and the oracles of Ormus which you wrongly find contradictory. They are far from being the work of impostors, and I come in God's name to confirm them to you. I tell you again, in His name, that the most accursed of all races will spring from your union; it will be the source of the most cruel calamities unless you quickly break the bonds that unite you. If you give up Syderia, your marriage will, on the contrary, be the prelude to the last day of the earth and the resurrection of all mankind. The outcome, one way or the other, depends on you. It must be one or the other: Ormus never intended it to be understood that both were possible at the same time.

Already, unhappy Omegarus, is not the first oracle of Ormus beginning to come true? What bitter fruits have you not garnered from the voyage undertaken on the orders of the Spirit of Earth? Must I remind you of the deplorable fate of Idamas, of the threat to you from the Americans, your hasty flight, the resistance and the struggles of Syderia, your remorse after the gratification of your desire, and the terror in which you already lived when I met you. Tell me, are these the brilliant successes the Spirit of Earth promised you?"

This pronouncement from Adam shone a fearful light into the mind of Omegarus. He tried in vain to turn away from it, but he could not stop thinking of it. Yielding to the full force of it, he trembled as he replied to the Father of Mankind, "You have just filled the cup of my misfortunes to overflowing, and I defy Hell to make them worse. My most cherished illusions are shattered, and I see before me the terrible truth by which I am condemned. I acknowledge my guilt and I seek to defend myself no longer. But I am not a barbarian — I will never consent to the death of Syderia. She shall live, and I shall see her again. If I am doomed to be the most wretched of men, she will wipe away my tears and will understand the cause of them. No! I will never abandon her. And you, ancient one, whoever you are, you will not prevail on me to do that!"

As Omegarus uttered these words with wild and distracted looks, his knees gave way and his voice faltered. Adam remained calm and answered, "If I were to tell you who I am, you would not dare to defy me in this way. Alas! It would have been sweet to open my heart to you, but I expected from Omegarus a greater willingness to obey the commands of Heaven, a more heartfelt repentance for his faults, and less weakness in misfortune. I was mistaken. You are not worthy to know me."

This reproach offended Omegarus and roused his curiosity. He began to examine Adam closely, and was surprised that he had not previously been struck by the dignity of his countenance — a grandeur that one would have sought in vain in any other human being. Deep lines scored his face, prominent muscles stood out on his transparent skin, his eyebrows had gone, and his head, quite smooth, shone like ivory. He might have been taken for the father of all the ages. An eternity of suffering had left its mark on his face; his looks knew no other expression but that of pain; and his only tone was one of melancholy. On his brow, however, withered and faded though it was, all the majesty of humanity commanded respect.

"If your name would have some ascendancy over me," Omegarus said to him, "to conceal it would be a crime greater than any of mine. I entreat you in the name of all the Heavenly powers to tell me who you are, or on the day when the Sovereign Judge pronounces sentence on me, I will rise up and blame you for all the disasters following on my resistance. Your refusal shall be my justification."

The Father of Men replied sharply: "I shall not give you that excuse, but woe to you if the name you demand of me does not effect a change of heart in you. Dear Omegarus, I was not able to conceal from you my emotion when you described the nuptial bower and the youth and charms of Eve in the arms of her too-happy husband. Oh! My son, you recalled for me the brief moments of happiness in my life. I am the unfortunate parent from whom you and the whole human race took their being." As soon as Omegarus heard the name of Adam, he flung himself at his feet as if he were in the presence of God Himself. Who could describe the turmoil of his emotions? Even though he was filled with veneration for the Father of Mankind, he had not forgotten that he had demanded the death of his wife and of the child in her womb. He could not hold back his sighs and deep sobs. His soul was like the sea when contrary winds drive the waves in all directions. Torn by a thousand conflicting emotions, he cried, "My father, what moments you make bitter with the poison of a single command!" He could say no more.

The Father of Men raised Omegarus and supported him in his arms, and, while he let the tears of Omegarus flow over him, he tried to console him. As the lily scorched by the fiery heat of summer which, when night comes with its cooling dews, revives, raises its head, and gleams again in silvery splendor, even so the words of the Father of Mankind assuaged the sorrow of Omegarus. The clouds vanished from his brow, and his soul, more composed, could listen to the language of reason and of virtue.

The Father of Mankind said to him, "My son, what grief you caused me with your imputation that I wished to break your heart, and would take pleasure in doing so — I who love you more dearly than I loved Abel; I who wished not only to spare you the pains you would inevitably suffer in this life but also wished to protect you from evils a thousand times more fearful: the punishments God reserves for disobedience. You are aware of the only misdeed I committed, and you will shudder to know the punishment for it. God ordered me to be placed before the gates of Hell, in an unknown land where I live in solitude, where I see no other human beings until divine justice has condemned them to the fires of Hell, and hear no human voices until the pit opens and their cries rend the air and pierce my ears. What a frightful torment it is, endlessly renewed, which will last as long as the earth endures. But you could bring it to an end today. Dear Omegarus, my son, have I not shed tears enough? Throughout the years of my torment, the hardest rocks have crumbled to dust, the rivers and the seas have evaporated drop by drop, and the brilliant vault of heaven has grown dim. Let your heart be moved by the sufferings of your father! Obey the commands of Heaven! Listen to the voice of conscience and to the prompting of compassion that urges you to help me. I have caused the misfortunes of my descendants; but, if I can prevent the birth of an accursed race, my sin will be wiped away."

This picture of the torments of Adam threw Omegarus into a state of great fear, and terror was visible in his movements and written on his face. He gazed with wonder and pity at the unfortunate being who had lived through such suffering. So moved was he that his eyes filled with tears. "Alas!" he said, "is it possible that a beneficent God could condemn a weak creature to such cruel torment? With this example before me, I may judge what torments His justice is preparing for me; but, like you, I shall know how to bear them. You wished to perish with the Mother of Mankind. Like you, I shall be faithful to Syderia; and were you in my place, you would be no less generous. I have seen it in your joy at the mere remembrance of your unfortunate wife."

This reply from Omegarus surprised the Father of Mankind. He remained silent for a moment and then spoke forcefully in words that the wicked do not have the courage to consider but will forever be a comfort to the just: "After the example of weakness I gave, I lost, my dear Omegarus, the right to give you an answer. But if you could only know the remorse I suffered the moment the crime was committed! It was as if a hungry vulture were constantly gnawing at my heart without being able to destroy it. If you could only see how every minute of every day through countless years I wished to be transported back again to the moment of my sin, to be master of my fate once more and resist the pleadings of a wife too dearly loved. These vain desires, which I could not suppress, consumed me. Crime is over in a flash; regret is eternal. It will accompany me even to Heaven where, if you will obey the counsels of virtue, your victory will place you in a rank above me and the greatest men."

"Oh my father," Omegarus replied, "I do not delude myself into thinking that I can attain such glory. Is it possible for men to attain such sublime virtue? I would rather be like you. I call Heaven to witness that I never thought that your fault was a crime; and I pardon it. Make the same allowance for me."

"It would be cruel to accord you such a favor," Adam replied. "In so doing, I would be your enemy, and the enemy of Syderia too. You think that in saving her you are showing your love. What folly! You would be delivering her to the wrath of a vengeful God, to the fury of the elements, to every earthly scourge, to the atrocities her children will commit when they plunge into her breast the weapon dripping with their father's blood. End your lives rather than live at such a cost. And what is death, the thought of which so terrifies you? For Syderia and for you, it would be the loss of a single day, the sleep of a single night. You would not have the time to go down into the tomb before rising again, clad in immortal robes, entering the true Eden, the abode of happiness and glory. Imagine that, at the same time, the ashes of your forefathers are restored to life, and the entire human race rises up and hails you as its benefactor. Will you be deaf to the prayers of all those who plead with you, through my voice, to hasten the day of their resurrection? They have been asleep in their tombs for countless centuries. Do you wish to prolong on earth the empire of woe and death? If the terrible consequences of my fault had been shown to me at the moment I was about to commit my sin of disobedience to the Eternal, I would not have caused such misery to my descendants."

The Father of Men, through whom God spoke, had delivered

these words so forcefully that the truth shone through with blinding clarity. Omegarus, his resistance overcome, vowed in his heart to obey. He raised his hands and with sorrowful looks offered up that great sacrifice to the only being who could reward him for it.

To the Father of Mankind, Omegarus replied, "Your cruel commands shall be obeyed. In consequence, I shall perish; but death is a blessing in the midst of so many calamities. I have only one wish. Could you refuse me this last consolation? If I abandon Syderia without telling her that I yield to the most imperious of commands, she will believe that I have ceased to love her. I shall become the object of her hatred. She will blame me for her death, and perhaps with her last breath will curse my love and the name of Omegarus. Allow me, my father, to dispel her error. I swear that, as soon as she hears from my lips the impediment which separates us, I will leave at once without waiting for her response and her farewells."

Omegarus scarcely had time to pronounce these last words, when Adam, knowing what he was going to say, raised his hands to Heaven and cried out: "Oh God! Man whom You created has not changed. I find him still just as I was myself, ever presumptuous in his promises, and ever the weakest of beings in his actions."

Then, he took the hands of Omegarus and said to him: "If you were to see Syderia again, she would ask to say only one word to you — to keep you for a single day. Would you be able to refuse her these small favors, you who are so eager to break my prohibition and the commands of God? Once the first day has passed without a dangerous incident, will it be any more perilous to stay with her for the next few days? Impunity will restore your temerity. You will accuse me of being a false prophet, and you will sleep easily on the edge of the most frightful of precipices. You promise steadfastness, it is true, and I do you the justice of believing that you say this in good faith. But you should learn to recognize your weakness. Absent though she may be, Syderia fights in your heart against your duty. She is stronger than your God, your own best interests, and your compassion for me. And you think you will be able to resist her when she holds you in her arms, trembling and weeping, and ready to die under the weight of her grief. Ah! far from Eve I would have died rather than break a single one of God's laws. It was her tears that were my undoing.[2] My dear Omegarus, you would never be able to escape the same fate. Finally, should Heaven give you the courage I lacked, who knows if it will not refuse Syderia the happiness of seeing you again, if it does not wish her to be ignorant of the command that separates you from her. My son, I beg you, do not be halfhearted in carrying out such a noble action. This is my last counsel to you. Divine justice now calls me back to the gates of Hell. Receive my final blessing. I go either to recommence centuries of torment or to see you tomorrow with the entire human race in eternity." The Father of Men made this pronouncement in funereal tones and then vanished from sight.

Omegarus remained motionless, deprived of all feeling — hearing nothing and seeing nothing. It was as if he were dead to the world, knowing not where he was or who had just been speaking to him. He knew only that he was unhappy and that returning to consciousness would be painful — a fearful sleep of the soul but less terrible than the awakening. By degrees, as the light returned to his soul, he felt his sorrows flooding back with all their original force. He raved and grew calm by turns; he despaired and wept; he regretted his pledge and was ready to go back on it. "I cannot believe," he said, "that God would be so arbitrary and cruel as to make the fate of the world depend upon my misfortune. Let Him manage the affairs of the world without me!"

Omegarus went out to brave all the dangers that had been foretold for him. He took the road to his dwelling, but his pace was very slow: remorse, weighing him down, slowed his steps. He felt that he had lost everything, even any hope of happiness. "Where am I going?" he asked himself. "I am to look for Syderia. Can I hope to find in her those charms I once worshiped, that tranquillity which innocence bestows, that happy calm I loved to see in her eyes, that joy she displayed in my presence — a joy that showed in her every movement? Alas! I am going to burden her with my remorse, my anxieties, my fate. I shall have saved her from death. But I shall see the poison of my griefs consume her slowly, and I shall hear her one day perhaps reproach me for my weakness."

Struck by the force of this thought, he stopped, and saw in the deep shade of an old oak tree the Father of Mankind. His face was marked with sorrow, his hands pressed tightly over his ears, his body bent double with the weight of his sufferings, his mouth wide open as if he were crying out. Omegarus heard him lament in these words: *"Centuries of torment begin again for me."* Omegarus was deeply moved and wept. At that instant, God allowed a vision of his descendants to be displayed before him.[3] On a barren plain under a dark sky he saw his hideous progeny, misshapen in form and cruel in disposition, making perpetual war on one another. He watched them seated around tables running with blood, heaped with the limbs of their brothers, fighting over the quivering remains which they devoured. He recoiled in shock from these revolting images, and swore obedience to God rather than give life to such an infamous race. Scarcely had he resolved on this course when Omegarus felt himself invigorated by new courage. He was ready to leave Syderia. But, before taking flight, he wanted to leave her a message in stone that would tell her of his innocence. To his right, he saw the remaining section of a fallen column. With the fragments scattered around its base, he raised an altar by the road, and using a sharp stone, he engraved upon it these words in large letters: *Omegarus is not guilty.*

When he had finished, he prostrated himself on the ground and addressed this short prayer to God: "Oh Thou who seest my suffering, if Thou dost reward the sacrifice that virtue demands, lead Syderia to this place so that she may read what is written here and not die without knowing the innocence of Omegarus. And you, Father of Mankind, whose torments I am about to cut short, and you shades of my ancestors who are asking to live again, support my faltering courage." Having said this, and without further delay, Omegarus took again the road to the French capital and abandoned Syderia.

CANTO viii

Virtue says to man: "Come to my altar and bare your bosom. I wish to sacrifice you." If he resists her commands, she punishes him instantly. She gives him over to the unending pains of remorse, and those pitiless executioners settle on their prey, pursuing it down to Hell. But, if he chooses to obey her commands, he scarcely has had time to form his intention, when grateful Virtue restores peace to his agitated mind, dispels the storm, and her voice, sweeter than that of any flatterer, heaps him with praises which the voice of Truth confirms.

Omegarus was surprised to experience instantly these benign effects. The impetuous rush of his feelings was arrested. Light began to break in upon him, and calm returned. He was able to question himself closely about his intentions. Pleased with the answers he received, he looked up to heaven with confidence; and he found consolation in the recollection of a God who controls the world. Let the angels sound the trumpet that is to awaken the dead, let the earth be destroyed and the light of the sun and the stars be extinguished — Omegarus could contemplate those sights with courage. He was worthy to witness the last day of the world.

Already portents of doom anticipated that event. Lamentations and mournful sounds rose from deep caverns and caves; many voices were heard groaning in the air; the leaves of the trees shook without any breath of wind; animals howled in fear and, taking flight, leapt over precipices. The church bells fell to ringing, moved by some unknown force, sending throughout the land their message of death as if they were tolling the funeral knell of mankind. The mountains gaped wide and vomited out clouds of flame and smoke. The ocean's waves grew dark. In the windless air, they rose up moaning, then crashed thunderously on the shore, flinging dead bodies everywhere. All the comets, which had terrified humanity since the days of creation, converged on the earth, reddening the sky with their terrifying presence. The sun seemed to weep, its face covered in tears of blood.

These presages did not deceive. The Almighty had written in the book of destiny that He would preserve the earth for as long as the human race had the power to perpetuate itself. He foresaw that Syderia would not survive the flight of Omegarus, and that the only fertile woman left on earth was going to perish. Released from His promises and from the laws He had imposed on Himself, God gave the signal for the resurrection of the dead. The heavens responded with sounds of rejoicing. Shudders ran through Hell, where the damned sought to hide themselves in the flames. The angels who stood before the throne of God sounded the trumpets of the last day, and the reverberations reached to the ends of the earth. Everywhere, in an instant, the remains of all human beings were revealed. To the north the ice opened to give them passage; and in the tropics, the boiling seas threw them upon the shores. The graves opened and they came forth — from shattered trees, split rocks, collapsing edifices. The earth resembled an immense volcano from which, through an infinite number of fissures, human bones and ashes were ejected.

When Omegarus saw the opened tombs, the bones issuing from the depths of earth, and human ashes scattered through the air, he was seized with terror. His hair stood on end, and he froze, for he feared to walk upon what seemed to be living dust. The undulating movement of the ground carried him along, as if he were sailing on the sea. Barely able to support himself, he clung to a tree. He clasped it in his arms, resigned to meet his end, like the sailor who, no longer able to fight against the storm, leaves his sails to the fury of the tempest and waits, pale and trembling, for the wave that will sink him or dash him to pieces on the rocks.

Three hours were enough for the resurrection of all human remains, so swift and violent had the eruption been. As soon as God, who knows the number of atoms in the universe, whose eyes can penetrate the deepest recesses of nature, had seen that earth had yielded up the ashes of mankind, He bade it rest. Then the ocean called back its wild and furious waves; the winds fell away, colliding with one another, and returned growling to their caverns. A mournful silence followed the global storm. Omegarus was astonished to find himself still alive; he dared not believe that peace had returned. He listened . . . No sound reached his ears. He left the tree he had been clasping and ventured to look about him at the objects surrounding him. He was filled with amazement. The earth was so disfigured that he could scarcely recognize it, as the departing human remains had shattered or destroyed those terrestrial bodies that had housed them. Here, mountains had lost half their foundations and seemed to be suspended in air. There, entire cities had vanished beneath the covering ashes. Everywhere, in all the burial places, frightening gulfs had opened. Not a tree, a plant, a rock, a building remained whole and entire; and all of them appeared in strange and frightening shapes.

At the sight of all these broken vessels, Omegarus raised his hands in thankfulness to heaven. It seemed to him a miracle that he was alive in the midst of a wrecked world. With every glance at the ruins surrounding him, he told himself that God had sheltered him under His wings. That thought cleared his mind of the terror that had oppressed him. He began to think that the shock was perhaps no more than the distant prelude to the resurrection of the dead. Already hope had returned to comfort him. He continued on his way and came to the place where once stood the capital of the French empire.[1]

There he thought to find shelter for the night, where he could recover from his painful experiences. How vain his expectations! How time brings changes to human affairs! Paris was no more. The Seine flowed no longer between its banks. The gardens, temples, the Louvre had all disappeared. Out of the large number of buildings that had once adorned her, not even a miserable hut remained where a human being could find rest. The whole place was a wasteland, a vast expanse of dust, home to silence and to death. Omegarus surveyed the sad scene and, seeing the heaps of ashes, was moved to say, "Is this all that remains of the proud city whose slightest movement shook the two worlds? There is not even a ruin, not even a solitary stone on which I could shed my tears. And yet I can fear to see the end of earth, that tomb of mankind and of all human institutions."

As he moved on, lost in his thoughts, Omegarus saw in the distance a statue that he had not noticed before; and he asked himself what marvel had preserved it intact when so many more durable monuments had vanished in the general destruction. His path led him to the feet of the statue. He approached and examined it. He reckoned that, judging from the various carvings that decorated it, the statue represented a former sovereign of France. The base was covered in inscriptions which he perused and read: "I was born beneath African skies. I wished to see Europe; and in passing by this place, I renewed the pedestal which time had damaged." In another place, Omegarus read: "Lima was my birthplace. Interested in knowing the second Athens, I found here this overturned statue. I had it raised up with the help of friends who came on this journey with me." Finally Omegarus read another inscription: "I am a sculptor, born on the banks of the Ganges. I made my camp for two months in this wilderness in order to restore this statue completely."

"That great man who is recorded here," said Omegarus, "must be very dear to posterity. Think of it! So many centuries gone by, and so many revolutions that have removed all memory of the world's once-dominant empires — they have not had the power to diminish the interest that this prince inspired. His statue, the object of devotion and love among men, has been preserved by their efforts. The human race has taken it into safekeeping, and all who pass this way have made it their sacred duty to repair it. I will not leave here without finding out about the hero represented in this statue."

Omegarus looked eagerly for his name. The lettering was barely legible; and when he managed to read it, he discovered that the name of his great man was Napoleon I. It was a name known to Omegarus. Indeed, he knew that this monarch was one of his ancestors. He raised his hands in respect toward him and addressed him: "Father! If it is true that the shades of the dead find comfort in the homage paid to them on earth, receive this tribute of the love and regard of men. It will be the last. Your name, however, will never be far from my memory." With these words he shed tears upon the statue of that great man.

Since the departure of Adam, it had not been possible for Omegarus to weep. Despair had dried his eyes; he was dying away like a plant that the heat of the sun had withered. The tears he now shed, sweeter than the dew, were a relief and comfort to him. His grief, now assuaged, no longer oppressed his spirit; and all that remained was the exhaustion from the struggles he had undergone. As weak as a sick man after a violent fever, he asked one last favor of Heaven: to lead him to some cavern or other shelter before night enveloped him in darkness.

His prayers were heard. As he left the city, in the riverbed where the Seine had once flowed, Omegarus came upon a solitary and simple house. On seeing the refuge Providence had given him, he felt a ray of hope penetrate his heart. Confident of a resting place for the night, he slowed his pace and stopped. He turned toward the west and gazed at his surroundings and the sun which had almost completed its course and was sinking beneath the horizon. This spectacle, which Omegarus had often seen with little interest, touched his heart. The thought came to him that perhaps the sun would not return to illuminate the world and would be extinguished forever in the ocean. He made his last farewells to the sun, and on behalf of the human race. He gave thanks for all the benefits the sun had bestowed on them in its daily round. And then, looking at the bones and the dust of human beings which covered the surface of the earth, he addressed these words to them: "How highly are you esteemed! This star, the most beautiful of God's works, which people worshiped as the Lord of the universe, is about to die while you will rise to eternal life on the ashes of extinct suns!"

As he was still speaking, the sun's disk vanished over the horizon, but the twilight no longer came as usual to console the earth for its absence. It was not that the sun had perished, but that its implacable enemy, Night, on seeing the approach of its last moments, had hastened to mount her ebony carriage. Joy shone in her eyes as she called on the shadows and said to them: "I know not whether you have forgotten your noble origins. As eternal as God, do you recall the time when I, with you, ruled unchallenged over chaos and space? Oh! Fatal day when God created the sun, and its first glance put me to flight. Since that moment I, who am the mother of repose, have known no rest. To what depths have I fallen! Subjected to the caprices of this fiery orb, I regained control of the heavens only after the sun had tired of its course. Even in repose, it still found pleasure in annoying me with the reflected light of its rays, and then soon reappeared to drive me ingloriously away. Darkness, my faithful companion, you who share my shame and pain, know that the reign of this arrogant monarch is coming to an end. Look upon the proud sun! In its triumphal career, it insulted all the stars, you yourself, and the whole of nature. See how grief has darkened its brow — its light is already dying. Let us hasten to finish off a dying enemy, and assume our rule over the firmament that is ours by right!"

At that, Night made a sign to Darkness that she was to follow her. No longer did she rise slowly over the horizon with the timidity of a slave who dreads to approach her master. She cleared the bounds of ocean with all the speed of her chargers and, in an instant, enveloped the heavens.

Omegarus, surprised by darkness, had difficulty in reaching the house he had seen. Nothing barred his way, and he went forward slowly into a dark vestibule which he inspected. Turning right into the adjoining room, he fancied he could see the glimmer of a light through a crack in the door. Could the house be inhabited? Would Omegarus find someone to console him in his sorrows? He opened the door, his heart throbbing with hope and joy. The place was lit by an ever-burning lamp, which men called an everlasting light. Opposite the door and above a bed, an old clock was still ticking and showed the time as nine in the evening. To the left, stretched out on a bed in a deep alcove, there was a dead body: it was the body of Tibes, the last occupant of the house. Near the bed, his wife lay in an open sepulcher. It was Tibes himself who had built this mausoleum to assuage his sorrows, a monument to grief which he covered with his tears. When it was completed, he placed there the embalmed body of his wife, and then he engraved on it these touching words: *We will be together in death.* From that moment, he had begun to pine away, and soon he felt his body's strength failing. Then he dared not leave the room lest death should strike him down far from his wife. Finally he expired on that bed — his only regret not to be buried in the same tomb with her. Omegarus examined the room carefully, stopping before the remains of Tibes who was no more than a skeleton. He contemplated the mausoleum and read the inscription. The words — *We will be together in death* — reawakened painful feelings in him. He read them a second time, his eyes brimming with tears. "Thus," said he, "I should have loved Syderia after her death and to my last breath. They were happy together, and they enjoyed a happiness that I have scarcely known."

Thereupon, Omegarus decided to investigate the house which he thought might still be inhabited — a hope he had not abandoned. He took the everlasting light and walked into the room where Tibes had assembled the principal works of the human mind. There, he had passed the happiest hours of his life, and there he had found consolation after his wife's death. Running his eyes over those books preserved from the depredations of time, Omegarus fancied he saw gathered before him the greatest men in the world. "So, these are the works," he said, "which men vainly have called immortal; and tomorrow, perhaps, they will be no more. Let the world vanish! I have no regrets for a dwelling that is falling to pieces; but I do weep over those books that the printing press has preserved, which are as fine now as they were when they were first published. Where, then, is the omniscience of a God who looks on the works of the human mind as nothing and consigns them to oblivion?"

Omegarus, undecided about accusing God of unnecessary cruelty, saw on the table a document which Tibes had written some days before his death. It contained these reflections: "Here on earth, nothing merits the regret of the wise man. Why should we preserve tomes about the earth and the stars which will soon be no more; about human beings, when their nature is going to change; about languages which will be spoken no more; about God whom the greatest intellects have not understood? What work can be more magnificent than the sun as it came from the hands of the Creator? It will perish. Why should God, who will not save His own works from destruction, preserve the works of man — man who is the crown of creation?"

Struck by these great truths, Omegarus remained confounded by the vanity of human affairs. The pettiness of human beings terrified him. He saw only God in the universe, letting his imagination paint a sublime picture of His greatness, of His dwelling place, and of the happiness He reserves for the just.

On coming out of the library, Omegarus went into a large room where the provident Tibes had accumulated many provisions which his skill and experience — those children of necessity — had taught him to conserve. As soon as Omegarus had recovered from his exhaustion, sleep overcame him, lay heavily on his eyelids, and let him inhale the drowsy scent of its poppies. Omegarus was about to yield to their influence when he remembered that he had seen a couch beneath the old clock. He went back to the room where Tibes lay, drawn by a fortunate presentiment, and he learnt that, during his absence, there had been some marvelous happenings. As he walked along, he felt agitated without knowing why his senses had been troubled. On reaching the entrance to the room, he was seized by a reverent fear as if he were entering the sanctuary of the Divinity. The first things to catch his eye were gold and azure clouds which gave out the most delightful fragrance, floating above the bed of Tibes and the coffin of his wife. Omegarus, who believed himself to be in the presence of God, advanced with a slow and hesitant step toward the bed of Tibes. He looked about for it. An astonishing sight met his eyes. Tibes had disappeared, and a young man had taken his place. Vibrant color glowed on his face; and the only indication of death was his total stillness. Omegarus could scarcely believe his eyes. He looked in the coffin to see if the wife of Tibes was still there.

She, too, had gone — or rather, like her husband, she had recovered the first flush of youth. Her flaxen hair lay in ringlets upon her bosom and was her only garment; a soft blush colored her cheeks, and a smile played on her lips. Everything about her spoke of slumber and pleasant dreams.

The Almighty had restored Tibes and his wife to life; but they were as yet without their souls. These wandered still in the place of shades, sad and unhappy, eager to revitalize the bodies from which they were separated, waiting impatiently for that happy moment. Omegarus could not take his eyes from Tibes and his wife. He imagined he saw them already rising together from the couch of death. He anticipated their ecstasy and their delight; and he wished he could witness such a happy sight. In this resurrection, he adored the hand of the Creator. He reckoned that the end of his sufferings was not far off, that at last all human bodies were thus changing, and that this night was perhaps dedicated to this end.

The old clock struck the last hour of day and roused Omegarus from his reverie. The solemn notes, sounding twelve times on the old timepiece, echoed through the shadowy silence and had a deep effect on him. He said in a doleful voice: *"The last day of the world is now beginning."* He remained still, lost in thought for some minutes, his eyes fixed on the hour hand of the clock, thinking that after time had devoured all things, it would end its reign and yield its place to eternity. Sadness took hold of his heart, for he was sensitive to the fate of so many human beings for whom the end was coming. He did not hide from himself that his last hour was approaching and that Death, ready to take him, was perhaps waiting for him to fall asleep. He imagined he saw him standing by his side, leaning on his scythe, covered in the blood of all mankind, and impatient to strike down his last victim.

The solitude of that place terrified Omegarus, and he trembled with fear. He felt that a man on the point of death has need of a companion to support him. The tears he shed brought him no relief. He wished that Syderia, guided by the Spirit of Earth, alarmed for his safety, would come running into his arms, even though all the calamities foretold by the Father of Men were to fall upon him. "But what wishes are these?" he said. "How could Syderia come here? All too well have I concealed my flight from her, and I have put too great a distance between the two of us. Alas! Maybe while I am talking, she is breathing her last." This image of the death of Syderia tore at his distracted and despairing soul. He turned his eyes to Heaven and made this prayer to God: "Oh Thou who hast preserved me on this dreadful day, I live but to suffer. Cut short my life, for my afflictions are more than I can bear. If Syderia still breathes, soften the pains of death for her. Show her in the mirror of dreams all I have suffered — my pain, my struggles, and my tears. I have hurt her too much to beg that she should still love me. All I ask is that she should die without hating the author of her sufferings. This is the desire of my afflicted heart. Deign, Oh Lord, to hear the prayer of the last mortal to address you. Wilt Thou reject the last prayer of the man who calls on Thee?"

As he finished these words, Omegarus looked down at the wife of Tibes. Serenity showed on her brow. The inner heavenly joy, which seemed to shine from her face, communicated itself to the soul of Omegarus. His sadness vanished and his spirit revived. He begged Heaven to forgive the murmurs which had escaped him; and, without wishing to hasten the actions of Providence, he fell into a gentle sleep.

CANTO IX

How diverse and admirable are the works of the Creator! And the earth is not alone in reflecting such variety. Mortals, lift up your eyes and consider the heavens, where a similar profusion is blazoned throughout the firmament. How myriad are the suns that burn in the sky! How endless are the movements that carry them through space! How different they are, despite their infinite numbers — differing in the orbits they describe, in their shape, and in their magnificence! Here are planets, covered in fruits and flowers, that are like delightful gardens, Eden-like worlds where the inhabitants appear like gods of nature. And there, ruined worlds roll through the firmament — sterile wastelands, masses of rock where venomous reptiles and savage animals fight with one another for their vile prey. More distant still are suns of immense magnitude, flaming furnaces ceaselessly pouring out torrents of light which flood through space. Elsewhere other stars, pale and almost extinguished, emit their last glimmers of light. Thus has God provided infinite variety for mankind.[1]

As soon as Omegarus had, in obedience to the Father of Men, resolved to leave Syderia, Heaven was moved by his submissiveness and began to alleviate his sufferings. In vain did a thousand perils threaten him during the destruction of the world; even the shattered remains of earth could not touch him. On his journey, he found a monument which told him in flaming characters of the regard posterity had for a hero who was one of his ancestors. Then an invisible hand led him to the house of Tibes where the Creator, who entered with him and in his presence, began the preparations for resurrecting the dead.

How different was the fate that Syderia experienced! Abandoned by Omegarus, without knowing why she was deserted, alone on the most dreadful day on earth, how rapidly did she encounter all degrees of human misery! If the hope of a better fate revived her for an instant, that false happiness immediately vanished, and her disappointed anticipations added to her woes. Her suffering was like that of the mariner whom the tempest has plunged into the boiling waves, who struggles to reach a fragment of his vessel, and at the very moment when he reaches out to grasp it, a raging wave sweeps him away and drags him down into the depths of ocean.

After Syderia had said farewell to her husband and to the Father of Men, she felt at once dark forebodings rising within her, warning her of the misfortunes to come. She regretted leaving her husband and, fearing that she had lost him forever, wanted to see him once again. Slowly she moved away from him, hoping that he would perhaps call her back. She was astonished that, in the presence of a stranger who did not know her, she lacked the courage to hear the tally of her failings. She reproached herself for her timidity. Whenever she felt on the point of going back to reveal the fears that agitated her, that same overpowering weakness held her back. As she came near her dwelling, she imagined that she was plunging into a sea of misfortune. She feared the future. She wanted to halt the fleeting moment as it sped on its way.

She entered the palace at that moment when the sun indicated the tenth hour of the morning. She prepared a meal for her guests in distracted fashion, as if her efforts would be in vain. Her mind was absent, away in the place she had departed. Confident that Omegarus was continuing the story of their love, she went on with the account which she imagined she could hear from her husband's lips. As long as this comforting illusion lasted, she felt herself at peace; but, as soon as she thought that the account must have come to an end, she became alarmed. Unable to remain alone in that dwelling, she paced ceaselessly on the terrace of the palace, where she looked repeatedly for Omegarus and called to him in vain. She worried about his continuing absence and exhausted herself in thinking of any causes for the alarming delay; and she began to feel anxious about that old man whom she had first regarded as harmless. She recalled fearfully his appearance in that uninhabited place, the singular character of his face and the various emotions it displayed — an inexpressible mixture of unease, severity, and compassion. Syderia did not comprehend why all these anxieties which then assailed her had not struck her before. For four hours she struggled with these fears; and it seemed an eternity. It was then that she despaired of her husband's return, and she resolved to go back there to confirm what she feared.

Syderia departed, and, in the course of her journey, her trembling knees gave way beneath her. Severely fatigued, she finally arrived at the grotto where the Father of Men had been sitting. Both had vanished. In an instant, she took in the entire horizon. Not a sign of Omegarus. Still she wanted to deny her fears. "Would he have abandoned me," she said, "I who lived for him alone, I who left my father, my country, and the companions of my youth to follow him? If some heavenly command, unknown to me, should have required that sacrifice from him, why did he conceal it from me and fly from me like a guilty man? His devotion to me had not diminished. Would he not have wanted to sustain my courage and comfort me with his last farewells? Would he have abandoned me to despair, to death, to the frightful suspicion of thinking him false? That I cannot believe. Omegarus may have taken another route to the palace — a path unknown to me, and maybe at this moment he is calling me and complaining of my absence."

She wished to go back, but before leaving that place, she looked about it more closely to see if there were any signs of Omegarus. Alas! Her fateful searching brought a revelation. Of a sudden her face grew pale, her head sank upon her bosom, and her eyes filled with tears. "He is gone!" she said. "He has fled from me. This I can no longer doubt. I can see his footprints on the ground, pointing in an easterly direction toward the French capital." Syderia did not have the strength to say more. Her eyes remained fixed on the footprints Omegarus had left; it seemed as if she would die gazing upon them. "He has gone," she said again. "What a mistake I made in thinking that he would have bid me farewell. The betrayer feared my grief and my tears; for he could not bear the sight of them. I would have swayed him, cruel though he is, or I would have fallen dead at his feet."

Syderia remained silent for a few moments, reflecting on various possibilities. "There remains but one thing to do," she said. "It has been only four hours since he left. His trail, which he cannot hide from me, can serve to guide me. I must pursue and overtake him. If it is true that he has deserted me, I will learn what are the crimes I have committed."

Thus she spoke, and, lighter than the winds, she seemed to fly on wings. Her eyes fixed on the footprints of Omegarus, she followed closely along the way he had gone. Soon she encountered the stone he had placed on the road and, drawing near, she saw newly written characters and recognized her husband's hand. She trembled in her joy, as if it had been Omegarus himself. She thought he was going to explain the reasons for his departure and allay the tumult of her spirit. She read the inscription eagerly. At first, the words *Omegarus is not guilty* did nothing to lighten the darkness of her mind. "I cannot understand the sense of this," she said. "But the message seems sinister to me. Omegarus asserts that he is not guilty; and I have not accused him of any crime. Was it not more appropriate for him to tell me where he had gone, why he had left, and if he means to return?"

Syderia read the message again and reflected deeply upon the words. Their gloomy meaning slowly dawned on her. "Ah!" she said, in the clutches of despair. "I understand only too well the dread meaning of these words. Omegarus has deserted me — the only crime he has committed, and the only one he fears I will hold against him. Perhaps he wants me to put the blame on the old man who accompanied him, or on Heaven itself. How can I tell? He leaves me prey to every kind of suspicion, and he is no doubt content if I believe him innocent. Think of it — at the moment of a painful separation that was his sole anxiety. He is not afraid to break my heart. His only fear was lest he should appear guilty in my eyes. Perhaps he thought that, when he pierced my heart, I would be the one to excuse and pity him!" And at this, she broke into floods of tears that did nothing to assuage her grief. "I would have done far better had I known nothing of the truth that I came to find. Unable to think that Omegarus had abandoned me, the hope of his return would have sustained me, and I would have awaited his return at some future time. Now, I have lost even that feeble hope that might have consoled me."

Her excess of grief left her paralyzed for some time. She remained silent and unmoving; but soon anger conquered her grief. "He is not guilty?" she said. "Was it not Omegarus who brought me into this wasteland which I loved for his sake? Was he not the one who has now left me without anything, without even a friend to wipe away my tears? Meanwhile, he knows that I will not survive his desertion, and that in consequence, before he left me, he had condemned me to death. These are his crimes, and he says he is not guilty!"[2]

When she had vented her wrath in this way, gentler thoughts came back to Syderia. The thought that Omegarus was guilty caused her unbearable pain. She grappled with this idea, wished to reject it, and to assuage her grief she wanted to believe her husband innocent. "Alas!" she said. "Am I sure that he fled of his own free will? Who can tell, while I am accusing him, that in some other place he is not bewailing our separation? Who knows that the old man is not a messenger from God and that he, with the help of the heavenly powers, obliged Omegarus to leave me without letting him tell me about our mutual misfortunes? How I dread lest the last words of Ormus could be coming true. God, who forbade our marriage, has perhaps released us from these fatal bonds! That is the entire and dreadful truth. Omegarus is no longer my husband, and there is no remedy for my misfortunes!"

She ceased reasoning and fell into the most gloomy silence. Her eyes were still transfixed by the traces of her husband's steps. "Heavens," she said, as tears filled her eyes, "these are now all that I have left of Omegarus. It is fortunate for me that these wild places are not inhabited, for I will not lose sight of his footsteps. I will follow after him and overtake him, as long as I still have a few hours of life in me!"

She tried to stand, but her grief had left her exhausted. Her trembling knees refused to carry her; she staggered and fell fainting on the stone that Omegarus had erected. Alone, without anyone to help her, was Syderia about to perish? How happy she would have been in her misfortunes, if death had then carried her off; for she faced the most dreadful awakening. She regained consciousness at that moment when the resurrection began, when everywhere the earth gaped wide open and hurled human remains into the air. Syderia did not know where she was. At times, she thought that sleep still held her in its embrace, that the upheavals she saw were illusions and fantasies. At times, she thought she was no longer among the living, that she had gone down to the realm of the dead, or that she was in some place close to Hell. Like a being restored to rational life, but not knowing her own identity, she searched her consciousness and memory to discover who she was and what her life had been. All in vain. She rose up. The stone that had served her for a bed caught her attention. She examined it and read again what was written. The words *Omegarus is not guilty* were for her a shaft of light that dispelled the darkness of her spirit. She knew who she was; all her misfortunes came crowding into her mind. "Alas!" said she with a sigh. "Would that Omegarus could have seen me almost dead here on this stone. Would he still say that he is not guilty?" She resumed her plan of following him in the midst of the universal upheaval and the many dangers she would have to encounter. She looked for the tracks he had left. But she had not anticipated being unable to find them. As the rising tide that covers the sand sweeps away the tracks of carriages and footprints of travelers left behind on the shore, so all trace of Omegarus had vanished. Here, they had disappeared into gaping earth. There, human ashes had fallen on them, covering them as winter covers the earth in a thick blanket of snow.

Syderia gave way to despair. In her frenzy, she took the first path she could find. She had no fear of being swallowed by the earth as it opened and closed around her. She had no fear of being crushed by falling buildings and trees. She rejoiced in the dangers that menaced her and wished only to die. As the bacchante, possessed by the god she serves, spear in hand, her hair streaming out, beats her breast and fills the air with her cries, so Syderia leapt over hill and precipice. She called ceaselessly on Omegarus. Submerged in swirling flames, she fell. Falling stone from collapsing buildings struck her. Blood streamed from the injuries she received, covering her face, her arms, and her garments. She was no longer that Syderia, the only woman in the world who could claim perfect beauty. She was so badly injured that Omegarus would not have recognized her.

Then, there came a calm that saved her life. This new tranquillity revived her courage and she hurried onward. Spurred on by her impatience, she managed to reach one distant object after another. The nearer the sun came to setting, the more she hastened onward. She wanted, like the sun, to travel the whole world in a day and embrace it all in her sight. Sadly she watched the sun dipping down below the horizon and vanishing before her eyes.

Syderia still hoped to enjoy the soft twilight that follows after the close of day; but she was astonished and dismayed to find herself enveloped in such profound darkness that everything was hidden from sight! She surmised that the Almighty, who was opposed to her plans, had commanded the Night to halt her progress. This thought discouraged her; for she felt the crushing despair that is born in a soul overburdened by sorrow and fatigue. She could not refrain from reproaching God with his severity; and, hoping she might die of exhaustion, Syderia continued her journey.

Still in sorrow, she had reached the summit of a high mountain, when she saw in the distance a feeble light shining in the darkness. On seeing this, abandoned hope was reborn in her heart. "Who," said she, "can be living in this place and awake at this hour? It is Omegarus — it is he, I am certain! Almighty God," she continued as she raised her hands to heaven, "I thank Thee for this blessing. It is Thou who hast brought me here. I was unjust in charging Thee with severity. Forgive me my transgression which my misfortunes should absolve in Thy sight. I ask only one favor of Thee. Give me the strength to reach this dwelling, for I shall be happy if I can see Omegarus and die in his presence!"

After this invocation, she moved toward the light which guided her; but she no longer felt the wild courage that no danger could diminish. She had become timid and shuddered at the least danger; despair no longer quickened her pace. She slowed her pace and conserved the strength which she regretted having wasted. She was so close to the house that she thought herself already there, when suddenly her limbs stiffened and she was paralyzed by excessive fatigue. Almost at the end of her journey, she despaired of ever arriving there. She wanted to call on Omegarus, but the sound died on her lips. Forced to take some rest, she sat upon the ground and wept. Then she offered this brief prayer to God: "Cease, Almighty Father, to pursue a weak creature. She may have sinned against Thee, but her innocent heart had no part in her failings. All I ever wished was to see Omegarus before I die, and Thou wouldst deny me this consolation at the very moment when I was hoping to enjoy it. I revere Thy will, cruel though it may be. If Thou meanest to cut my thread of life, and make me drain the cup of suffering, then strike now, for the measure of my misfortunes is overflowing."

It seemed as if this prayer brought her comfort and that God, moved by her sufferings, restored her strength. Syderia stood up with a painful effort and dragged herself slowly toward the dwelling where she saw the light shining. She stood before it and knocked on the door. The knocking reverberated through the darkness. At that hour, at the finish of that most terrible day, it sent a wave of fear through the building. The silence was profound. She knocked again, repeatedly and with greater force. Then she saw the light change position and move toward her. This alarmed Syderia, and a thousand feelings — joy, fear, hope — rose within her. "He is coming," she said. "It is he." The door opened and a man with a torch in his hand appeared, followed at some distance by his trembling wife, half-hidden behind him. They were Policletes and Cephisa, who had been hosts to Omegarus on his first journey. They had been so frightened by the eruption of human remains that they had not dared to surrender themselves to the sweet balm of sleep, and they remained wide awake in their fear. Syderia's knocking on the door had increased their terror. Policletes thought that the dead had risen from their graves and were asking for hospitality. In vain, Cephisa begged her husband to refuse them shelter. He rose up, and when she sought to stop him, he said, "These dead were once human beings and, if they are unhappy, it is my duty to help them." The sight of Syderia — pale, dejected, disheveled, and covered in blood — confirmed them in their beliefs. They took her for a specter returned from the infernal regions, and they did not dare to speak to her. Syderia, deceived in her hope of meeting Omegarus, remained speechless with grief. She was on the point of entering the house of Policletes, but, fearful of receiving help that would prolong her life and her sufferings, she fled into the sheltering darkness. Thus were those words accomplished which had been spoken to Policletes: the end of his fearful apprehensions would be near, when he should see the wife of Omegarus without recognizing her.

Syderia was overwhelmed by the weight of her misfortunes. Scarcely had she made a few steps into the city of Policletes, when she felt the chill of death creeping over her. Believing that she had no more than a moment to live, she went into a nearby temple whose doors had been demolished, and she sat down on the steps of the altar to breathe her last in peace.

That was at that same moment when Omegarus was raising his hands to Heaven in the house of Tibes, and begging God to mitigate the sufferings of his wife. His petition touched the Almighty who, seeing Syderia lying on the steps of His altar — alone, and in the clutches of despair — was moved with pity for her fate. He caused a poppied drowsiness to descend on her eyes, and He bade the angels who watch over the sleep of mortals to call up pleasant dreams for her. They obeyed and gathered around Syderia, presenting her with a thousand happy images in the mirror of dreams. Syderia thought herself borne away to a delightful valley where the trees were loaded with golden fruit and with flowers that gave off the sweetest scents. Seated at the entry to a delightful arbor was a young woman who rose to meet her, looking at her with the eyes of a loving mother. She pressed her to her bosom, and said: "I am Eve to whom God has restored the bloom of youth. My Daughter, I owe this happiness to your husband. Dry your tears. Tomorrow you will ascend to Heaven at his side."

The High Priest, Ormus, followed after the Mother of Men. He appeared to Syderia as he had done on the Plain of Azas, surrounded by all the inhabitants of Brazil. He was standing on the steps of the altar where the marriage of Omegarus was blessed. His brow was unclouded, peace was in his aspect, and a smile was on his lips. He said to Syderia: "Omegarus rebelled against my last commands and against the will of Heaven; but, in leaving you, he has made full amends."

In another vision, the great scene of the Last Judgment unfolded before the eyes of Syderia.[3] To the sound of pealing trumpets, which she thought she could hear, all the graves opened instantly and from them came without cease so immense a number of people that the startled imagination could not conceive how the earth had been able to support and feed them. Some shook off the dust and ashes which soiled their faces and their bodies; others hastily tore off their shrouds and flung them far away. The sailors, drowned at sea, were cast upon the shore where they were astonished to find themselves restored to life. Water streamed from their nostrils, from their hair and their clothes. They shuddered on seeing the ocean, seemingly still afraid of the element that had been the cause of their death. All the dead spread out across the earth, which no longer had space enough to contain them. Many of those restored to life were impatient to leave their tombs, held back as they were by the mass of bodies blocking their monuments and their burial grounds. Then God spoke to the seas of the two worlds and commanded them to disappear; and, hearing Him, they vanished. A great multitude soon filled the empty chasms, packed more closely together than the cornstalks that gild the fertile plains. And then God commanded the earth to provide more space; and at once the mountains were leveled; the earth's surface increased and became an immense plain covered by all the human beings who had ever lived.

Syderia marveled to see so many descendants of Adam, myriads of them numbering more than the stars in the sky or the grains of sand on the shores of oceans. It seemed to Syderia that God would require innumerable centuries to judge them all; but a single instant was enough for Him. He commanded that the veil hiding the conscience of the dead should fall away, rendering it visible as the sun on a cloudless day when its light covers the whole world. All the guilty were confounded to see their sins and remorse revealed to the sight of all. With bowed heads concealed behind their hands, they hastened to hide their feelings of guilt. All in vain — their arms, hands and heads, every part of them, became clear and transparent. Their first torment was to stand before the righteous whose gaze they could not bear. The parricide fled from the father he had killed; the corrupt judge from the innocent he had condemned; the adulterous wife from the trusting husband she had deceived. All the wicked fled away; and all the righteous, in their turn, shrank with horror from the hideous sight of those consciences stained by evil deeds. The just sought out the just, and the wicked sought out the wicked. No convulsion in nature — neither the waves in the midst of the tempest nor the dreadful clash of opposing armies — nothing could adequately convey the turmoil of those who sought and fled from one another. The just hastened to the east, and the wicked to the west. Soon their division was complete.

Syderia saw Omegarus in that spot lit by the rays of the rising sun. He was surrounded by the just who stretched out their hands to him in thankfulness, for they perceived in his soul the sufferings he had accepted in order to hasten their day of glorification. At his side, Syderia saw the old man she had seen the day before. His face was radiant; and his eyes shone with joy. She could not repress a feeling of hatred; for it seemed as if he still wished to keep her away from Omegarus. Breaking through all barriers, she flung herself into the arms of Omegarus, who embraced her and said: "Oh Syderia! How many misfortunes are forgotten in so sweet a moment!" Hardly had he spoken those words, when lightning lit up the sky, peals of thunder sounded, and the Almighty, followed by His angels, came on clouds of gold and silver to pronounce the Last Judgment. At one glance, He took in that immense multitude of human beings. He perceived that they had already passed judgment on themselves: that the just had gathered in the east, and the wicked in the west, each according to the scale of their virtue or their iniquity. The wisest of mortals were assembled nearest the east; and the most evil, who feared to face those less guilty than themselves, had hastened to hide themselves in the west. Thus, according to the places they had chosen, their scale of wickedness or of goodness was revealed to all. All that remained for the Almighty was to punish or to reward.

He made a sign and commanded that the bodies of the just were to become lighter than the most subtle vapor; and immediately losing the weight that bound them to earth, they rose up into the heavens. Syderia ascended with Omegarus, as the wicked trembled with rage to see the triumph of the just. The earth shook and disintegrated beneath the feet of the wicked, and they fell with her into a vast furnace of sulfur and flame. Syderia wept to see their fate, guilty though they were. She would have put out those fires which burned without consuming. She wished she had not witnessed their pains, for she feared that those dreadful sights might disturb her happiness; but the angel who watched over her sleep caused her to forget Hell and the tortures of its inhabitants by opening up the heavens for her to see.

She gazed in total ecstasy, for she experienced most vividly a feeling unknown to mortal man — purest happiness and absolute peace together in the happy union that Heaven reserves for the just. On earth, joy and peace are ever separate; for happiness is always hedged about by the cares and troubles of life; and peace brings with her weariness and boredom. Only in Heaven are peace and happiness conjoined. Syderia spent the last hours of the night basking in that heavenly happiness. She wanted it to last forever, but it would last no more than a moment for her.

CANTO X

The earth was on the point of destruction. Nothing could preserve her, save only the efforts of the Spirit to whom God had entrusted the care of watching over her. In fact, this ever-active Spirit still possessed great power: he ruled the elements, and he knew all the secrets of nature. All he had to do in order to prolong the existence of the world was to return Syderia to her husband, or to keep her safe together with the child in her womb.

At the moment when the dead emerged, he was at the center of the earth, in the workshops built by him which stretched from pole to pole. His immense laboratory was a repository of all human knowledge; for there he had assembled all the tools, a variety of machines whose uses were known only to him, and every entity to be found on earth or hidden beneath it. There, on innumerable shelves, he had placed bronze vessels in which were stored the sap and seeds of plants and the various essences of animals. It was here that, ever since the Creation, the indefatigable Spirit had been bringing together the elements of all bodies. There, he interrogated nature and compelled her to answer him. From these caverns, there came precious discoveries which were attributed to chance or to human inventiveness, when in fact they were gifts from the Spirit. There, in millions of furnaces, he maintained perpetual fires for the heat that held back the deadly cold which was advancing day by day to the center of the world.

Of a sudden, the Spirit heard deep down in his caverns a widespread booming sound, a general and confused commotion. He watched in astonishment, as swarms of atoms streamed out of the bronze vessels, and the bodies that surrounded him rose up to the vaulted roofs of his caverns, opened a passage, and disappeared from sight. In a vain attempt to halt them, he ran to lower the heat in the furnaces which he thought too fierce. He did not know the cause of the phenomenon. He was troubled in mind, the prey of gloomy thoughts. Unable to remain any longer in those subterranean chambers, he sprang up to the peaks of the Pyrenees. From those lofty mountaintops, he saw waves of dust emerging, growing in size every second, and forming into a dense cloud which obscured the surface of the globe. When he made a close examination of these deposits which the earth was sending forth, he realized that they were the ashes of humankind. He froze in terror, grew feeble, trembling and undecided. "What!" said he. "Are Omegarus and Syderia dead? Is this the prelude to the resurrection?" As he spoke, he saw on the shores of Hesperia Death leaning on his scythe, contemplating with a tranquil eye the eruption of human ashes. The Spirit hesitated, uncertain about approaching Death, for he had held no communication with him since he had slain, by the hand of Cain, the firstborn of the children of men. The mere sight of Death roused his fury, for he saw him as the sole cause of the death of mankind, the destruction of the earth, and of all the calamities that threatened the world. Yet the Spirit wished to learn from Death whether Syderia and her husband were still alive; he wanted him to save such dear creatures since their lives were the guarantee of his own. There was so much at stake that he abandoned the hatred he had thought implacable, and he drew near Death. Hiding his desires and his fears, the Spirit questioned him courteously, asking whence he came and whither he was going. Were there still great numbers of human beings alive on earth? Above all, had his terrible scythe struck down Omegarus and Syderia? Death answered that, from the time when he had struck down the High Priest Ormus on the Plain of Azas, he had not left America; and there, feeling that preparations for the Last Day obliged him to do so, he had just exterminated the inhabitants. He went on to say that Omegarus and Syderia were still alive, and that he was moving on to Europe in order to complete the extermination of the human race.

This intention alarmed the Spirit, and he spoke against it in these words: "You do not expect that some beneficent stars could one day draw near the earth to restore it and return it to its primal state?" Death replied: "They would be too late. Man cannot reproduce himself; the human race is extinct." To that, the Spirit answered: "It still lives. Even though this revelation should prove my undoing, we shall see if you are so much your own enemy as to kill the last hope of the earth. You should know that Syderia carries a child who may yet become the father of a new race." With a look of contempt, Death replied: "You are like those decrepit old men who promise themselves many years of life, even though my scythe rests on their heads. Gaze about you. Look at these clouds formed from human ashes. Look far off and see those plains white with the bones of the dead. Look at the seas that everywhere are casting the dead ashore. Would you have the power to halt this resurrection now in progress? Believe me, the end of all things is at hand; and so I yield to my destiny." The Spirit answered: "What weakness in a being whom I knew once to be so strong, who brought on his own misfortune by destroying mankind. Have you forgotten that, on a mountain in Asia, God gave me His word to preserve the world for as long as men were able to increase and multiply? Spare Omegarus and Syderia who have this power; and the Almighty will cause these ashes and these bones to return to their graves on sea and land rather than break His promises." "I have no desire," Death added, "to prolong a sad old age. My vigor declines day by day; and I have changed so much that I no longer recognize myself. In past times, like the Almighty, I was present everywhere and in the selfsame moment I struck down my victims in all parts of the globe. Nowadays I can scarcely cover the different parts of the world; and I can no longer find anyone to strike down. My thirst for blood torments me — a desire that I cannot satisfy."

The Spirit answered: "Would you be happier to return to the nothingness of chaos, enchained for an eternity of time? Do you consent to the happiness of all those creatures you have destroyed, who will defy your powers by returning to eternal life. Put away such shameful thoughts. Rather than act on them, assist me in my plans. We have the same interests. If it is written that we are to succumb to the blows of Almighty God, we will know at least a glorious defeat. It is true that you are bent under the weight of ages, and that your strength is beginning to fail. Know, however, if the primal springtime returns to earth, you will recover with her your old strengths. Oh Death! You will once more have the earth in your power. Men will again fill the earth with their numerous posterity, born to perish beneath your onslaught. You will again recover your role as Death with the glittering scythe that never rests. You will enjoy a new empire over mankind, which will endure for so many centuries that it will seem like an eternity."

This speech of the Spirit proved convincing for Death, who was seduced by the hope of regaining his youth and his powers. He stayed some time with his somber thoughts, and then, breaking the silence, he said to the Spirit: "Without trusting completely in the hopes you hold out, I would agree to support you. I swear that I will spare Omegarus and Syderia as long as they shall keep alive the flame that makes love fruitful. I know them both, and I know their dwelling. Begone! Go back to the center of the earth where your labors summon you. You can trust the word of one who, ever inexorable, now relents for the first time." And with that, they parted.

Death went on his journey to find Omegarus and Syderia on whom the Spirit had built such high hopes. He raced rapidly through Hesperia, cleared the Pyrenees, and advanced to the banks of the Rhine. There a few human beings dragged out a miserable existence, still terrified by the universal eruption. Death at once put them out of their misery. Then, moving on toward the site of the French capital, he appeared over that region of Europe at the hour when Night folds her veil and surrenders the heavens to the chariot of Dawn. Death was not far from the house of Tibes. His piercing eyes, penetrating the deep gloom and the triple walls, perceived that there were living creatures in the dwelling. He hastened there with the ferocious rapacity of a starving eagle that dives down on the timid lamb. As soon as he entered the room, feelings of fear and respect, entirely foreign to his experience, arose within him. Astonished, he halted for a few moments, and then he moved on toward the bed of Omegarus, who was lost in a deep slumber. Surprised to find him there, Death looked with pleasure on the beauty of his face touched with an indefinable and heavenly majesty. "And this is the new Adam," said he, "who is to be the father of many children." That thought caused him to rejoice at the hope he might kill them one day.

The absence of Syderia left him uneasy; and, as he looked about for her, his eyes fell on Tibes, who seemed to be still alive. He went up to him and, thinking to seize him, found pleasure in saying in his treacherous way: "While this young man is asleep, I will cut his thread of life." And three times he raised his scythe to cut him down; and three times the murderous weapon dropped from his hands. At that Death was terrified. "Who is this youth," said he, "whom Heaven requires me to preserve? Is this an angel in the guise of a mortal?" Looking at him more closely, he was startled to discover it was Tibes whom he had killed on that same bed. "What!" he continued. "Has Tibes already donned immortality? Has the resurrection commenced in the midst of silence and the shadows of night?"

Death peered into the coffin where the wife of Tibes lay. At the sight of her, in the bloom of first youth like her husband, he said in angry tones, "Either the Spirit is himself deceived or he has tricked me. My reign is over. Should I spare Omegarus? Let him perish!" he went on, gazing on him menacingly. He brandished his terrible scythe and was on the point of striking the deadly blow, when a gleam of hope, the recollection of his oath stayed his hand. And, fearing to break his word, he fled from the house of Tibes.

Sad and dejected, he continued his journey toward the west of France, moving, though he knew it not, to the spot where he would meet Syderia and the Spirit of Earth. Darkness still covered the world. Death was astonished to see that the sun had not appeared over the horizon. In his disquiet, he continually looked back toward the east, thinking that the sun would never return to shine upon the world. He was wrong, however. The sun had only slowed in its cycle, as if it feared to show itself to our degenerate, decaying, dark world. At length, the sun finally appeared, but so changed that human eyes could no longer recognize it — the disk indistinct and darkened, abandoned by the dawn, who no longer went before in her triumphal chariot. The sun no longer had the power to outshine the faint light of the stars. Seen together, the sun and the night stars were a frightening spectacle. Unfeeling though he was, Death was moved by the sight: earth's God on the point of death. "It will not cover the half of its course," he said. "It tells me that earth has no more that a few hours of existence. How senseless I was to believe the words of the Spirit. Despite so many examples from mortals which tell me to ignore the siren voices of false promises, I too have been the dupe of hope." The thought filled him with shame. He was infuriated by his weakness, and he swore to have his revenge on the Spirit who had deceived him.

Meanwhile the promises of Death had in no way diminished the anxieties of the Spirit of Earth. When he departed from Death, he had for no more than a moment tasted the delights of having diverted him from his purpose; for dark forebodings suddenly flooded his mind. He felt that his courage and his reason had gone from him, and that his attempts to recover them only served to increase the fear and disorder in his soul. He went back to his subterranean caverns; for he thought that in his powerhouse he would find relief for his distress. There, however, everything ran counter to his hopes and served only to drive him to despair. Under those dark and gloomy arches, he heard groans and saw specters stalking about. He wished to return to his labors in order to control his fears; but his tools broke when he touched them, and the fires went out when he sought to blow life into them. "Who can say," he said, "what misfortunes these sinister presages foretell? Let us call upon the demons of Hell. Once they calmed my agitated mind when the waters of the Deluge covered the earth, when the ocean separated America from the ancient world. Maybe they will give me the repose and peace for which I search in vain."

In the middle of a deep cavern, he had cut a grotto out of the rock and adorned it with the shells of sea monsters. Here he had raised an altar to the infernal spirits, made of black marble in the shape of a tripod. An ever-burning sepulchral lamp threw a gloomy light on it. Above the altar there was a picture, painted with human blood, which showed the rebellious fiend at that moment when Eve, seduced by his words, timidly took the fruit of the forbidden tree in her hands. Joy shone in the eyes of Satan and in the treacherous smile he gave, even as he tried to hide his delight.

The Spirit came to the foot of the altar, holding in his hand six serpents which raised their hideous heads with fearsome hissings. He placed them on the altar, took a sword, and cut them into a thousand pieces. As the tainted blood poured from the reptiles and covered the altar, he made this prayer to the infernal spirits: "Oh you, whom I have never invoked in vain, come to my aid! I am threatened by fearful and unknown dangers. Tell me what is happening on earth, in the celestial regions, and in the depths of Hell. Be my guide. Inspire me with a course of action, for I cannot grasp what is transpiring. If my fears are correct, then I am approaching my last day, and the destruction of the world is at hand. Join with me in preserving the world; it is yours as well as mine. Take the treasures I have hidden in my caverns; and take the secret of my power. I give myself entirely unto you."

As soon as the Spirit had concluded his prayer, the caverns shook under his feet, trembling like the leaves of the trees when the wild North wind blows. Those subterranean depths echoed and re-echoed with thunderclaps which were repeated from pole to pole. The great arches of the caverns opened, as legions of demons from every corner in the grotto rushed in, while the Spirit, eyes flaming and hair on end, continued to conjure them up. No sooner had they all come together, when they all, with one voice, cried out wailing and lamenting: "We are returning to Hell!" And with that, they departed with frightful howling. Suddenly the light in the grotto went out, the picture over the altar was rent in two, the altar itself was shattered, and the grotto turned to dust.

In his terror, the Spirit of Earth thought that Death had broken his oath, and that the traitor had just sacrificed Omegarus and Syderia. He saw that God was the only power in nature who could save the world; but, when the world began, the Almighty had set a term to his existence. The more centuries he lived, the less could the Spirit resign himself to death. Every second of his life increased his will to live.

He paced through the caverns, considering various plans that he took up and rejected one after the other. "Should I not blush at my cowardice?" he said. "I am afraid to die, I who have seen men, those weaker creatures, face death and accept their end with courage. Death? It was not death, for they knew very well that they would be reborn to immortality. They knew that their spirits would outlive their mantle of clay. Death, it is not you I fear. It is nothingness that fills me with horror. All the human beings I have seen, all will rise again to eternal life. As for me, I shall be no more: I have no eternal life before me. A dreadful thought which I cannot bear. "Oh God!" he groaned. "Do with me as it pleases Thee. Cast me down to Hell. I would rather burn with the demons than suffer annihilation."

The Spirit did not have the strength to go on. The words died on his lips; his heart grew heavy; he staggered and fell. He suffered the most extreme agony. A sweat of blood, in color like the complexion of an African burnt by the sun, ran across his face, streamed down his body, and darkened the ground. The violence of his fit shortened the duration. The pain decreased, but his anxieties continued to increase. "I cannot live!" he said in torment. "I must know if my misfortunes are inescapable, and if Omegarus and Syderia are still alive."

He left his caverns, went to the palace where they dwelt, went into every room without finding them, and came away in haste. He searched the places nearby with more care than the eager hunter who goes after the stag he has lost, leaping into valleys, flinging himself from the high mountains, going into cottages and hovels, down to places underground, into every building that could hide a living creature. In the end he found Syderia on the steps of the altar, where sleep had released her from her sorrow; but it was a Syderia he hardly recognized, so greatly were her features disfigured.

He was impatient to know who had brought her to that place,

what could have separated her from her husband, and what could have destroyed her youth and her charms. So he dissipated the perfume of poppies which had sent her to sleep. Syderia woke up, and the heavenly delight that filled her soul vanished with her awakening. It was not without pain that she came back to the life from which she thought she had been delivered. Not wishing to be surprised by day in the town of Policletes, she rose up and hastened away, wishing to return to the places she had left by the same road she had followed the previous evening. She gave up, however, her intention to look for Omegarus, for a single night had changed her aspirations. She no longer doubted that all the events which had made her desperate were entered in the immutable decrees of Providence. She resigned herself to the will of God, hoping only to end her days in finding the happiness that was prefigured during her sleep.

Unseen by Syderia, the Spirit of Earth kept pace with her. On seeing Syderia, whom he thought had joined the dead, the Spirit despaired no more of the salvation of the earth. "I possess," he said, "secrets that in an instant will heal the wounds of men. I shall have no difficulty in restoring her lost charms. I shall locate Omegarus, and eventually I will be able to reunite husband and wife." While pondering these ideas, and as he was thinking of appearing before Syderia in human form, he caught sight of two things that filled him with terror: the rising sun, almost extinct, and an enraged Death intent on fearsome projects.

The moment had come when the destiny of the earth, of Heaven, and of Hell would be settled forever. The last scene in the history of the world was beginning. The heavenly powers descended on clouds to witness the event. The shades of the dead, fugitive and wandering, hastened to the final scene. The infernal spirits halted the torments of Hell; they opened the gates and advanced to the dark threshold of their fearful dwelling place.

With slow steps, Syderia came down the mountain which dominated the town of Policletes. She had climbed it with painful effort the night before. Death saw her without knowing who she was, and, still thirsting for human blood, he leapt towards her, waving his murderous scythe. The Spirit perceived the danger and hurled himself in front of Death in order to stop him. Death continued on his way without giving him a glance. "Death!" the Spirit cried in a voice of fear, "What are you doing? Are you going to kill her? Do you not recognize Syderia?" And Death said with joy: "It is sweet to know it is Syderia. What pleasure I shall have in destroying her before your eyes!" With a cry of despair, the Spirit answered: "Have you forgotten your solemn oath?" And Death replied: "I have sworn to preserve Syderia as long as she can nourish the flame of love in her heart. I never promised to spare her when she is at the point of death, longing for the moment when I cut the thread of a life which is no more than a torment for her. Come! Learn from a woman how to die. It will prove a valuable lesson for you!" As Death was speaking, Syderia moved in front of him, her face calm and serene. Death did no more than touch her, and Syderia fell dead at his feet.

All Heaven waited on this great event with impatience; and there came an instant, universal cry of joy. The reign of time had ended, and a vista of eternity opened up. At the same moment, however, howls of rage arose from Hell, and the sun and the stars were extinguished. The dark night of chaos covered the world; plangent sounds came from the mountains, rocks and caverns, as all nature moaned and wailed. A doleful voice echoed through the air, crying out: "The human race is no more!"

The eyes of the Spirit which, like those of Death, have the power to see through the darkness, remained fixed on the body of Syderia. It seemed as if he wished to deny his misfortune in seeking to discover whether there was a spark of life still remaining. But those sinister words — "The human race is no more" — sounded in his ears and caused him to abandon his fruitless searching. In the end, he accepted that she was no more and that he, too, was about to die. His entire being changed: his mouth ceased breathing out flames, emitting nothing more than dense black smoke. He was lost and frantic. The sight of Death, who seemed to be watching his suffering with malign pleasure, added to his rage. His greatest torment was his inability to punish the treachery of Death. Darting furious glances at him, he spoke these words: "Barbarian!" he said, pointing to Syderia lying lifeless on the ground. "How could you cut the precious thread of her life? The whole human race was in her, and you have destroyed it with a single blow. This is the blow I have feared ever since you struck down the firstborn of men. I foresaw that, going from one murder to another, you would end by killing the last member of this unhappy race. Are you not appalled by the extraordinary importance of your victim? You have struck your blow, and you stay cold, without feeling; and yet all nature has cried out to reproach you for your dreadful crime. The mountains, caves, and rocks — every atom in the world laments as if you destroyed them in killing Syderia. There remains only one last crime for you to commit: kill me, and complete your acts of parricide. Already I can see your eyes ablaze with anger — you have a burning desire to shed my blood. Strike! But be warned that I shall know how to protect myself."

Death scorned the threat of the Spirit, and answered: "Do you dare to charge me with the crime of destroying the human race? God created you to preserve it, and he created me to destroy it. The two of us have obeyed the law given to us. What lies behind your anger, however, is that by shedding torrents of blood I have proved the greater benefactor of the human race. Had I not saved earth from an overabundance of children, they would have exhausted all her resources. I could have acted against you only by leaving them in the narrow space of this world where, crowded into every corner, they would have produced nothing, not even the barren weeds of the field. It was essential to slow down this growth of population, to destroy men in order to preserve the human race. Yes! Had it not been for me, the end of the world which you dread would have happened long ago. You are indebted to me for the innumerable centuries of your dominion."

The Spirit was on the point of replying, when Death broke in and said: "We are talking too much. I have never had the gift of persuading mortals, nor were they able to move me. I have to carry out the sentence that God pronounced on you when the world was created.

Do not attempt any futile resistance. Summon up your courage. You cannot win the fight against me." And as soon as Death had spoken, he raised his scythe to the full reach of his long arms in order to fell him with one mighty blow. As for the Spirit, silent and sorrowful, he watched closely the actions of Death. And, when he saw he could no longer stop the fatal weapon from striking his head, he leapt aside. The scythe missed its mark, cut through the air and fell upon the ground. Ashamed to have missed his prey, Death shook with rage, waved his deadly scythe in fury, and raised it again. The Spirit was terrified, thinking that this time he would not escape the fatal blow. He called for help to the winds, to the flames, the thunder and all the elements, but they were deaf to his cries. Flight was the only possibility he had left. He plunged into the earth and took refuge in the greatest of his caverns. There, he had for centuries assembled an immense amount of sulfur, bitumen, inflammable liquids, and that powder invented by the demon of war. There, despair in his heart, a torch in each hand, he awaited the pursuit of Death who was not slow in coming. As soon as he saw him, he cried out: "Halt! Move one foot and I will set fire to these explosives which I have assembled. I shall destroy the earth and entomb myself in the ashes. Then you will rule over a ruined kingdom."

Death gave no answer, and continued to approach him. Suddenly the Spirit flung his torches about the cavern, which immediately caught fire. There was then a tremendous explosion. The earth shook, was blown out of orbit, and was torn asunder. The Alps and the Pyrenees rose up, flinging huge masses through the upper reaches of the atmosphere. The Spirit thought that Death, terrified by these events, would not dare to attack him in the middle of the eruption where the fierce flames served as a barrier. A pitiful defense against Death! "You may be buried," he said, "in the deepest pit in Hell, but you will not escape me." And that said, Death flung himself into the midst of the flames, and pierced the Spirit who fell, uttering a cry that echoed round the world. On the death of the Spirit, the dark clouds vanished from the earth. A pale light, softer than the stars of night and brighter than the sun, gilded the vault of heaven without need for any other illumination. It was the dawn of eternity.[1]

I desired to see the conclusion of these marvelous scenes, to know above all the fate of Omegarus, to see the resurrection of humankind, and God sitting in judgment on the multitude of human beings. But the Spirit of Futurity refused me. "Man will never be satisfied," he said. "If I were to show you the scenes you long to see, your curiosity would still not be satisfied. You would want to look beyond eternity, if there were anything more to discover. I wished only to let you witness the triumph of Omegarus, and to show you that, by obeying the commands of Heaven, he will one day cut short the reign of time and hasten the coming of eternity. My mission is accomplished. Tell men about this history of the last age of earth. Sacrifice to this glorious task your hopes of fortune and your ambitions; and I will make the hours of your labors the sweetest moments in your life."

Albrecht Dürer, *Apocalypse: Seven Angels with Trumpets* (1498).

Preface to the Second Edition of
Le Dernier Homme (1811)

PRELIMINARY OBSERVATIONS BY THE NEW EDITOR

The name of M. de Grainville was familiar to me, but I knew of his talent and his works only by reputation. By chance, the present volume came into my hands, and I read it for the sake of an author whose great misfortunes and great virtues commend him to all men of sensibility. The fate of this work astonished me. The first edition was launched in obscurity — not a single reviewer, not a single man of letters deigned to advocate it in the face of public indifference. I except from my stricture the English scholar who, in a passage as well conceived and written as his interesting comments on Horace, has since spoken of M. de Grainville with an enthusiasm that does honor to both of them.* If it is true that it was a Frenchman who first revealed Milton's genius to the English, Sir [Herbert] Croft has chosen to emulate him in the most laudable manner. I like to think that our literature, which has already profited greatly from his vast knowledge, will feel especially indebted to him for this interesting discovery.

Moreover, after considerable reflection, I believe I have uncovered the cause of the public apathy that greeted *The Last Man* when it first appeared. It was published very soon after M. de Grainville's death from a manuscript in some disarray, and without preface or introduction. Some readers saw it as a mere romance, and when con-

---

*Horace éclairci par la ponctuation, par le chevalier Croft. Paris: Ant.-Aug. Renouard, 1810, p. 78, 79, and 80.

sidered in that light, it was at the mercy of readers incapable of judging it. Other readers must have seen in it the outline of a great epic poem — an epic which, as it stood, left much to be desired by exacting literary critics. I am convinced that, if the true circumstances had been known at the time of its publication, the public reception of this work would have been quite different. M. de Grainville had conceived the idea for *The Last Man* at the age of sixteen. He was still working on it, to the exclusion of all else, when he died in terrible circumstances. The published work was no more than a magnificent first draft that he had started to put into verse.** What we read there is all that remains of a man whose greatness goes unrecognized — a man lost to literature through an appalling calamity. I am convinced, I repeat, that if these facts had been known, M. de Grainville would have been assigned a place in literature which I hesitate to determine exactly, but which an enlightened sensibility would perhaps have placed not far below that of Klopstock. Readers will judge for themselves.

I say again, it is not for me to assign ranks in this great hierarchy of the republic of letters where I myself am a stranger. But the feeling that prompts me to do so — this need for justice which leads those of generous heart to insist on due recognition for an unfortunate and forgotten talent, this respect inspired by those of modest genius who are lacking in public glory — this is my excuse. Who could quarrel with this?

Now that I am reasonably certain of having found a kindred spirit in the reader of M. de Grainville, I will say to him: "How would you regard the man who, after so many centuries of poetry which has created such a profusion of marvels, found himself seized by an idea never before expressed — an idea that poetry had not anticipated? What would you say to a noble and sublime vision that would juxtapose the glorious days of the earth in its youth, as Milton described it, with the decadence and sickness of a dying world, the ill-fated

**The first canto was finished. I have had it in my hands.

loves of our last descendants with the delights of earthly paradise, and the end of all things with their beginning? What would you think if the poet had the skill — by a means as simple as it was ingenious — to present this entire epic saga as an account given by the *Last Man* to the father of the human race? I believe that this invention alone ranks it among the finest examples of epic inspiration. And what if this amazing tale of the imagination were to be articulated in the most natural and interesting manner within a fantasy genre that was hitherto unknown? Finally, what would you say if, in this rough draft not intended for publication, the reader were to find on every page the most well-crafted phrases, the most brilliant similes, the most remarkable descriptions? If so, you would still have no more than a feeble impression of the work of M. de Grainville. Once again, let readers judge for themselves.

M. de Grainville, envisioning only the grand outline of his poem, had not yet included many episodes. There are some, however, which appear to me to offer a kind of beauty that will not be lost on people of sensibility and good taste. There is, for example, the intervention of the Spirit of Earth, so appropriate to the theme; the resurrection of Tibes and his wife; and above all the homage paid by the *Last Man* to his ancestor before the latter's monument amidst the convulsion of the earth in her final disintegration. This last scene seems to me to contain the most subtle praise and — if you wish — the most sublime eulogy of the prince in whose day M. de Grainville was writing. It was certainly an episode of no potential profit to the author since M. de Grainville dedicated his tribute to the EMPEROR*** just a few days before his own death — that is to say, at a time when his long-accustomed suffering had led him to expect nothing from men or good fortune.

He no doubt understood that certain parts of his poem were somewhat inferior to the others. He would have removed some unsuitable episodes, some dull passages, some weak writing and over-

***Pages 86, 87, and 88 of the second volume [canto VIII].

blown phrases. A novice writer could have done it. I would have done it myself, but I respected even the faults of such a writer. And critical opinion will surely do likewise.

Have I any doubts about it? M. de Grainville left nothing to his widow but a name that posterity will perhaps someday cherish. On his behalf, I plead for such a legacy.

Ch. N.[1]

NOTES

NOTES TO THE PREFACE

1. I. F. Clarke, *The Pattern of Expectation, 1644–2001* (London: Cape, 1979), 45. The fake passage appears in *The Last Man; or, Omegarus and Syderia: A Romance in Futurity* (London: R. Dutton: 1806), 1:83, found on pp. 88–89 of the 1978 Arno Press reprint.

Another striking example of enlargement and embellishment appears in the following addition to the French version (1805 edition, 2:159), marked in italics, which was clearly intended to heighten the drama of the final episodes (2:187–89):

The great arches of the caverns opened, as legions of demons from every corner in the grotto rushed in, while the Spirit, eyes flaming and hair on end, continued to conjure them up. No sooner had they all come together when *the chief spirit of the regions of darkness pronounced the following words in a lamentable and anguished voice: "We appear before you, summoned by your powerful spells. Willingly would we promote your designs, and extend the reign of crime and iniquity. Hear and tremble. A mightier command than that of Satan, even the behest of the Almighty, constrains us to return to hell, there to be eternally employed in pouring the lava of heaven's wrath on the heads of those condemned by our seductions."*

The spirit ceased, and with the most hideous yells his declaration was confirmed by the host of attendant fiends. The Genius sank upon his face in an agony of disappointment, and, before he recovered the infernal demons had vanished, the light in the grotto went out, the picture over the altar was rent in two, the altar itself was shattered, and the grotto turned to dust.

2. The book carried an advertisement, "Just published, in 4 vols.," for a romantic tale titled *The Saracen; or, Matilda and Melek Adhel: A Crusade Romance.*

3. How did the translator come to misapply *granivorous* (*OED*: "That feeds on grain"), so rare a word that the *OED* can offer only four instances between 1646 and 1848?

4. The missing passage is located on 2:86 of the 1805 edition, beginning with *Tandis qu'il marche* and ending at the bottom of p. 88 with . . . *la statue de ce grand homme*. The passage will be found in our translation in the eighth canto, beginning with "As he moved on, lost in his thoughts" and ending with the sentence "With these words he shed tears upon the statue of that great man." Here are other examples of this careful pruning of French references: *descendent sur l'empire français non loin de la demeure d'Omégare* (1:19) becomes in the anonymous translation of 1806 "alighted on a great empire not far from the residence of Omegarus" (1:19) — where both France and the French vanish; *La France ainsi que l'Europe n'étoit plus qu'une vaste solitude* (1:33) becomes "Europe declined till it became one vast solitude" (1: 35); and *Je vois ses pas imprimés sur la terre et tournés vers la capitale des Francais* (2:113) becomes "I perceive his steps marked on the sand, and turned towards the East" (2:129), where the French capital disappears entirely from the text. For the brief reference to Joan of Arc, however, the translator improves on the original *brûla l'héroïne qui sauva la France* (1:44) with "burnt the heroine whose virgin arm saved France" (1:46).

5. See the entry for "Nodier (Charles)" in Pierre Versins, *Encyclopédie de l'Utopie, des Voyages extraordinaires, et de la Science-Fiction* (Lausanne: L'Age d'Homme, 1972): "Polygraphe et érudit français, 1783–1844."

NOTES TO THE INTRODUCTION

1. Poul Anderson, "After Doomsday," *Galaxy*, Dec. 1961 and Feb. 1962, reprinted as *After Doomsday* (New York: Baen, 1986); J. J. Farjeon, *Death of a World* (London: Collins, 1948); Glenn Kleier,

The Last Day (New York: Warner, 1997); Thomas M. Scortia, *Earthwreck* (New York: Fawcett Crest, 1974); William Dexter (William Thomas Pritchard), *World in Eclipse* (London: Peter Owen, 1953).

2. Gore Vidal, *Kalki*. (London: Heinemann, 1978), 189.

3. Aldous Huxley, *Ape and Essence* (London: Chatto and Windus, 1949), 94.

4. Harry Martinson, *Aniara: A Review of Man in Time and Space*, adapted from the Swedish by Hugh MacDiarmid and Elspeth Harley Schubert (London: Hutchinson, 1963), 129.

5. M. P. Shiel, *The Purple Cloud* (Aylesbury, Eng.: Panther Books, 1969), 129–30.

6. H. G. Wells, *The Time Machine*, ed. Frank D. McConnell (New York: Oxford University Press, 1977), 96–97.

7. An excellent study of the early period of future fiction is Paul K. Alkon, *The Origins of Futuristic Fiction* (Athens: University of Georgia Press, 1987).

8. *The Reign of George VI, 1900–1925* (1763), ed. I. F. Clarke (London: Cornmarket Reprints, 1972), xxi.

9. Ibid., 99–100.

10. Sébastien Mercier, *Memoirs of the Year Two Thousand Five Hundred*, trans. W. Hooper (Philadelphia: Dobson, 1772). Also Sébastien Mercier, *Astraea's Return; or, The Halcyon Days of France in the Year 2440*, trans. Harriet Augusta Freeman (London: n.p., 1797). For a comprehensive publishing history of *L'An 2440*, see Everett C. Wilkie, "Mercier's *L'An 2440*, Part I," *Harvard Library Bulletin* 32 (winter 1984): 5–35, and "Mercier's *L'An 2440*, Part II: Bibliography," *Harvard Library Bulletin* 32 (fall 1984): 349–400.

11. Sébastien Mercier, *L'An deux mille quatre cent quarante* (1786), 1: 114.

12. Peter Haining, *The Dream Machines* (London: New English Library, 1972), xviii.

13. Mercier, *L'An deux mille quatre cent quarante*, 2:190.

14. There are accounts of Grainville's life in Alfred Touroude, *Les*

Écrivains havrais (Le Havre: Librairie de E. Touroude, 1865), and in C. M. Le Roy de Bonneville, *Étude biographique et littéraire sur Cousin de Grainville* (Le Havre: Imprimerie Lepelletier, 1863).

15. This oath was the *serment civique,* an oath of loyalty to the Constitution, as set out in the *Constitution civile du clergé,* voted by the Constituent Assembly on 12 July 1790. This transformed all clergy into state functionaries. Bishops and priests were to be elected by those on the roll of citizens; the religious orders were dissolved. Only seven bishops out of 160 took the oath, but about one-third of the priests subscribed.

16. Jules Michelet, *Histoire du XIXe siècle jusqu'à Waterloo* (Paris: Michel Lévy Frères, 1875), 3:91–109. See also "The Secularization of Apocalypse" in Alkon, *Origins of Futuristic Fiction,* 158–91.

17. Thomas Babington Macaulay, *The Miscellaneous Writings, Speeches and Poems of Lord Macaulay* (London: Longmans, 1880), 348–49.

18. Two passages from the first chapter in *Les Ruines* have substantial echoes in Grainville's first canto:

The Arrival: Arrived at the city of Hems, on the border of the Orontes, and being in the neighborhood of Palmyra of the desert, I resolved to visit its celebrated ruins. After three days journeying through arid deserts, having traversed the Valley of Caves and Sepulchres, on issuing into the plain, I was suddenly struck with a scene of the most stupendous ruins — a countless multitude of superb columns, stretching in avenues beyond the reach of sight.

The Apparition: I thought I saw an apparition, pale, clothed in large and flowing robes, such as specters are painted rising from their tombs. I shuddered; and while agitated and hesitating whether to fly or to advance toward the object, a distinct voice, in solemn tones, pronounced these words . . . Confused with this discourse, and my heart agitated with different reflections, I remained long in silence. At length, taking courage, I thus addressed him: Oh, Genius of tombs and ruins! Thy presence, thy severity, hath disordered my senses; but the justice of thy discourse restoreth confidence to my soul. (Constantin-François Volney, *Les Ruines . . . des empires* [Paris: Desenne, Vollan, Plassan, 1792], 2–4).

19. A. Creuzé de Lesser, *Le Dernier Homme: Poème imité de Grainville* (Paris: n.p., 1831); Elise Gagne, *Omégar, ou Le Dernier Homme: Proso-poésie dramatique de la fin des temps en douze chants* (Paris: n.p., 1859). There is an excellent account of these versions in Alkon, *Origins of Futuristic Fiction,* 184–91. See also the entries for Gagne and Grainville in Pierre Versins, *Encyclopédie de l'Utopie, des Voyages extraordinaires, et de la Science-Fiction* (Lausanne: L'Age d'Homme, 1972), 353–54, 374–76.

20. *Private Letters from an American in England to his Friends in America* (London: J. Almon, 1769), 11. The book must have been successful, since a second edition appeared in 1781 with the changed title of *Anticipation; or, The Voyage of an American to England in the Year 1899, in a Series of Letters, Humorously Describing the Supposed Situation of This Kingdom at That Period.*

21. Quoted in Robert Dingley's exhaustive and most informative article "The Ruins of the Future: Macaulay's New Zealander and the Spirit of the Age," in *Histories of the Future: Studies in Fact, Fantasy and Science Fiction,* ed. Alan Sandison and Robert Dingley (Basingstoke, Eng.: Palgrave, 2000), 15–33.

22. Anna Laetitia Barbauld, *Eighteen Hundred and Eleven* (1811) (Warrington, Eng.: Sunrise Publishing, 1911), 39–40.

23. Horace Smith, *Poetical Works* (London: Henry Colburn, 1846), 1:234.

24. Eugenius Roche, *London in a Thousand Years* (London: Colburn and Bentley, 1830), 61.

25. H. O'Neil, *Two Thousand Years Hence* (London: Chapman and Hall, 1867), 9. The New Zealander's most notable appearance was the solitary figure in Gustave Doré's last full-page illustration, suggested perhaps by Blanchard Jerrold in his and Doré's *London: A Pilgrimage* (1871). Another appearance of the New

Zealander is in H. C. M. Watson's *The Decline and Fall of the British Empire*, published anonymously in 1890. It opens with yet another letter, from Melbourne, dated 12 August 2992. It begins: "My Dear Jack, You will, I am sure, be pleased to hear that I have decided to publish the story of my visit to the cradle of our race in 2990."

26. Mary Shelley, *The Last Man*, edited with an introduction and notes by Morton D. Paley (Oxford: Oxford World's Classics, 1998), xxi.

27. *The Battle of Dorking* was first published in *Blackwood's Edinburgh Magazine* in May 1871. The author was Lieutenant-Colonel Chesney (1830–95), later General Sir George Tomkyns Chesney, member of Parliament for Oxford. He was a distinguished officer of the Bengal Engineers, recalled from India in 1870 to establish the Royal Indian Civil Engineering College at Staines in Middlesex. From 1881 to 1886 he was a senior member of the government of India. He had never written more than occasional reviews before *The Battle of Dorking*. A full account of the *Dorking* episode will be found in I. F. Clarke, *Voices Prophesying War* (Oxford: Oxford University Press, 1992), 27–56.

28. J. A. Mitchell, *The Last American* (1889) (London: Gay and Bird, 1894), 21.

NOTES TO CANTO I

1. Zenobia, Queen of Palmyra, fought the Romans for the control of the Eastern Empire in A.D. 270–72.

2. The priestess of Apollo, known as the Pythia, was seated on a tripod and answered questions, usually about future events.

3. The unknown traveler of the first paragraphs rapidly becomes the control and continuity for the entire narrative. He receives his validation and his foreknowledge of the last things from the Spirit of Futurity. Knowing everything that is to come, he relates the succession of events, especially in the last two cantos, while the principal characters limit their own accounts to the episodes in which they were involved.

4. The old man who gazed "at the fragments of a broken timepiece and two blood-stained wings" is Time, often represented as a winged figure or with a winged head.

1. In canto I, the first appearance of Omegarus as the Last Man (from omega, last letter in the Greek alphabet) suggests that Grainville may have intended to give his characters an allegorical dimension. This seems to be confirmed by the appearance of Syderia (*sidéral:* heavenly). But that first impression is not supported by the entry of Policletes and Cephisa: there are no connections for this couple, and nothing discernible for Idamas, Palemos, Ormus. It is possible that Philantor may derive from the French *philanthrope;* but it is unlikely that Eupolis has any link with the comic poet of that name, a contemporary of Aristophanes.

2. Grainville here exploits the opportunities of the internal narrative within the main narration. The eyewitness account from Palemos is typical of the way Grainville authenticates his story with an "I-was-there" report from one of the various actors in the continuing drama.

3. Balloons were a familiar marker in future fiction after the first manned ascents in Paris on 23 November 1783. The earliest French use was in the theater: love-in-a-balloon plays like *Le Siècle des ballons* (1784). The earliest in English was the anonymously published *The Aerostatic Spy; or, Excursions in an Air Balloon* (1785): a rudimentary anticipation of Verne's *Around the World in Eighty Days* (1873).

1. Grainville's geography is deliberately vague but with some classical recollections. Their air machine seems to be following a course across Spain to the Fortunate Isles, off the west coast of Africa and not far from the entrance to the Mediterranean. These charmed isles appear in the *Odyssey* and were noted by

Cicero and Plutarch. Evidently the balloon is high enough for the travelers to see where England had been — delightful thought for French readers in 1805 — and to see the Mediterranean ahead of them. In Greek mythology, Alcmene was the daughter of Electryon, king of Mycenae, and the wife of Amphitryon. She was the mother of Heracles by Zeus. The Pillars of Hercules were one of the many enterprises of that hero. He parted the two peaks, Gibraltar and Abyla, on either side of the Straits of Gibraltar.

2. The notion of "a span to human life" is an early and telling example of the future-thinking that finds the shapes of coming things in the discoveries and inventions of the present. See, for instance, a most accomplished example in *The Time Machine*, where Wells draws on T. H. Huxley's theory of divergent evolution for the Eloi/Morlocks divide and on the entropy proposition of the German physicist Rudolf Clausius for the dying earth and the huge red sun seen by the Time Traveler.

Grainville made a similar imaginative leap from the known to the probable in his ideas about the balance between world population and human fertility. These derived directly from two important pamphlets of 1798. In June of that year, Edward Jenner published his *Inquiry into the Causes and Effects of the Variolae Vaccinae*, which promised an immediate end to the scourge of smallpox. Thomas Malthus followed three months later with his most influential *Essay on the Principle of Population as It Affects the Future Improvement of Society*. In a few incisive phrases, he introduced the world to the crucial difference between population growth reckoned in geometrical proportions and the increase in subsistence which came in arithmetical proportions — in other words, too many mouths and not enough food.

For the anonymous translator of *The Last Man*, Grainville's statement was not good enough. The French original was therefore amended with an English addition about "the profound improvements making in medical science, by which the lives of thousands of the infantine world have been snatched from the empire of death" (1806 edition, 1:83).

1. The last of the French have crossed the Atlantic, "the great ocean," and arrived in Brazil. In Grainville's geography, impoverishment and declining populations decide the shape of the political map. His Brazil, for example, seems to be the entirety of South America, the last of the great maritime powers; and his City of the Sun, in no way related to the Taprobane of Tommaso Campanella's *Città del Sole,* is a ghost town, a solitude without inhabitants. It is 100 miles from Cartagena. Can that be the port on the Caribbean, northeast of Panama? And where is the Plain of Azas, which does not appear in any gazetteer? Grainville says as little as possible about past history and world geography in order to increase the sense of the marvelous and to give more space to the extraordinary events in his story.

2. Aspasia, a famous courtesan from Ionia, was the mistress of Pericles. Laïs, a celebrated Greek courtesan, Sicilian in origin, brought to Greece at the time of the Athenian expedition to Sicily, was the mistress of Alcibiades. Semiramis was a legendary Assyrian princess of great power and beauty; Gabrielle d'Estrées, the mistress of Henri IV of France.

3. Nature, Night, Aurora — these are personifications which Grainville begins to use more frequently, since the increasingly dramatic action of the narrative lends itself to this animation of natural forces and abstract ideas.

4. The Tupics were South American Indians, originally inhabitants of the lower Amazon and Brazilian coast south to Uruguay; they were slash-and-burn cultivators, fishermen, and hunters.

1. The war between the French and the British in 1805 carries over into the text. Grainville begins by removing England from his-

tory and then goes on to give the French the glory of the leading role in his sacred drama. The anonymous translator of his
Le Dernier Homme, however, takes action in the British interest.
In the English version of 1806, he removes most references to
the French who now appear as "the strangers."

NOTE TO CANTO VI

1. The romantic, often amorous dalliance in this canto is clearly
designed to engage the interest of a more general readership.
Grainville develops a theme of pursuit and resistance. His presentation of the two paintings later in the canto is an interesting
solution to a problem: how can Syderia invite the consummation of their marriage without appearing too forward? Eve
offers an object lesson by showing "a blushing modesty mingled with the pleasure of yielding to her husband."

NOTES TO CANTO VII

1. There are echoes of the *Dies Irae* in these opening passages.
God appears to his servant, Adam, "in swirling rays of light" as
Rex tremendae majestatis. In Grainville's fictional portrayal, God
is infinite and eternal, "unchanged since those first days of crea-
tion when He revealed himself to Adam in the Garden of
Eden."

2. Grainville records the traditional belief that Adam's disobedience followed from his uxoriousness: "It was her tears that
were my undoing." The serpent tempted Eve to eat the forbidden fruit of the Tree of Knowledge ("Ye shall be as gods"), and
she "gave some also to her husband who was with her, and he
ate it." The central theme is obedience to the will of God, in
the beginning and in the end. As Adam puts it: "If the terrible
consequences of my fault had been shown to me at the moment I was about to commit my sin of disobedience to the Eternal, I would not have caused such misery to my descendants."

3. An ancient tradition held that God revealed to Adam all the future generations of humankind. The first major source for this

belief is in the apocryphal Book of Enoch, written at various times in the period 300–150 B.C. The revelations begin in the first chapter, where Enoch is presented as "a righteous man, whose eyes were opened by God that he might see a vision of the Holy One in the heavens, which the angels showed me, and from them I heard everything and I understood what I saw, but not for this generation, but for the remote generations which are to come" (R. H. Charles, *The Book of Enoch* [Oxford: Clarendon Press, 1885], 1:1–2). In chapters 83–90, there is an apocalyptic vision of the entire future to the last judgment and the resurrection. This foreknowledge was said to be conveyed in the original language spoken by Adam and the angels. The Elizabethan astrologer and mathematician John Dee (1527–1608) spent many years and much money in trying to discover this lost language.

NOTE TO CANTO VIII

1. In sentiment and in language, Grainville echoes a classic passage in Volney's *The Ruins* (London: J. Johnson, 1795), 12: "Who knows but that hereafter some traveler like myself will sit down on the banks of the Seine . . . who knows but that he will sit down solitary, amid silent ruins, and weep a people inurned, and their greatness changed into an empty name?" This opening leads on to a nicely turned celebration of France and of Napoleon Bonaparte. Travelers from the most distant countries have come to see "the second Athens," and they pay their respects to "That great man," whose statue is "the object of devotion and love among men." By 1805, Napoleon was at war with Britain, Austria, Russia, and Sweden. He was already well on his way to expanding his empire throughout the European continent, having recently won his greatest military victory at the Battle of Austerlitz. But, that same year, he also saw his naval ambitions destroyed by the British naval victory at the Battle of Trafalgar. Given these historical circumstances, it is therefore understandable (albeit reprehensible) that all references to Na-

poleon would be excised from the anonymous English version of *The Last Man* published in 1806.

1. The praise of God running through this opening passage is modeled on the *Benedicite,* a canticle Grainville would have repeated every day as a priest. The immensity and diversity of the universe proclaim the infinite power of the Almighty in preparation for the apocalypse about to follow. Space, planets, Eden-like worlds — these were familiar matter in eighteenth-century astronomy. As Cotton Mather (1663–1728) wrote in his *Christian Philosopher: A Collection of the Best Discoveries in Nature* (London: E. Matthews, 1721), 19: "Great GOD . . . How stupendous are the Displays of thy Greatness, and of thy Glory, in the Creatures, with which thou hast replenished those worlds! Who can tell what Angelical Inhabitants may there see and sing the Praises of the Lord! Who can tell what Uses these marvellous globes may be designed for!" The idea of the plurality of worlds attracted enduring interest especially after the immense success of *Entretiens sur la pluralité des mondes* (*Conversations on the Plurality of Worlds*) by Bernard le Bovier de Fontenelle (1657–1757). This international best-seller was published in French in 1686 and appeared in English translation in 1688.

2. Once Omegarus has, "in obedience to the Father of Men, resolved to leave Syderia," there is little left for him save to wait on the will of God. The action perforce concentrates on Syderia, who attracts the reader's sympathy as she searches for Omegarus, wonders about his intentions, and imagines the worst. She experiences the full gamut of emotions: anger and compassion, hope and fear; terror and tranquillity. And then she takes the reader with her through the last stages of a burning, collapsing world.

3. Grainville's description of the Last Judgment follows the sequence set in the *Dies Irae:*

Tuba mirum spargens sonum,
Per sepulchra regionum,
Coget omnes ante thronum.
Mors stupebit et natura,
Cum resurget creatura,
Judicanti responsura.

The visions that follow to the end of this canto are the promise of final, heavenly happiness for Syderia.

NOTE TO CANTO X

1. Grainville closes his narrative of the Last Man by acknowledg-
ing the infinite power and justice of God, and by presenting
Omegarus as a savior figure whose obedience "cut short the
reign of time." Grainville concludes the story where he began
— with the nameless narrator and the Spirit of Futurity. In the
opening paragraphs, the narrator suggests that he has had a
special guidance: "I know not what secret inspiration guided
me." And, for the rest of the story, the narrator tells the tale —
directly in his own words or indirectly through the accounts of
the principal figures — in order "to reveal to the world this history so worth telling." The narrator ends by wanting to know
more, but the Spirit of Futurity makes a neat conclusion by re-
fusing: "Man will never be satisfied." How true!

Did Mary Shelley borrow from Grainville in her own tale of
The Last Man? There are parallels between the opening pages
of *Le Dernier Homme* and the five-page introduction to Mary
Shelley's story. The narrators explain how they have arrived in
"that fearsome cavern" and in "the gloomy cavern of the Cu-
maean Sibyl." Both advance in spite of the warnings of their
guides, and both receive a revelation of future things: from the
foreknowledge provided by the Spirit of Futurity or the history written on the Sibylline leaves. The last word has to be —
a remarkable coincidence.

1. Charles Nodier (1783–1844), one of the "fathers" of French Romanticism, was a librarian, novelist, poet, journalist, literary critic, lexicographer, and *homme de lettres* at the beginning of the nineteenth century. In addition to his being the author of many works of nonfiction, he is perhaps best remembered as one of the pioneers of the *fantastique* in such stories as "Smarra" (1821), "Trilby" (1822), "La Fée aux miettes" (1832), "Hurlubleu" (1833), and "Inès de las sierras" (1837) as well as his early stage adaptation of Polidori's *Vampyre* in 1820.

   Nodier knew Sir Herbert Croft far better than the reference to "the English scholar" in his preface suggests. The baronet had settled in Amiens in 1807 and had employed Nodier as his secretary, bestowing on him 400 francs a month, an apartment of his own, two servants, and a carriage for visits to Paris. By June 1810, however, Croft found himself in financial difficulties, and Nodier asked to be released from his contract.

   In 1824 Nodier was appointed librarian of the Bibliothèque de l'Arsenal, where he established one of the most famous *cénacles* (literary salons) for the young Romanticists of the period. Victor Hugo, Alfred de Musset, and Saint-Beuve were all indebted to him. He was elected to the Académie française in 1833 and, among his other scholarly activities in this august body, was a prime contributor to the sixth edition of the *Dictionnaire de l'Académie française* (1835). There is a most informative account of this "polygraphe et érudit français" and his contributions to speculative fiction in Pierre Versins's *Encyclopédie de l'Utopie, des Voyages extraordinaires, et de la Science-Fiction* (Lausanne: L'Age d'Homme, 1972), 629–32.

BIBLIOGRAPHY

Ahearn, Edward J. *Visionary Fiction: Apocalyptic Writing from Blake to the Modern Age*. New Haven: Yale University Press, 1996.

Alkon, Paul K. *Origins of Futuristic Fiction*. Athens: University of Georgia Press, 1987.

Armytage, W. H. G. *Yesterday's Tomorrows*. London: Routledge, 1968.

Barbauld, Anna Laetitia. *Eighteen Hundred and Eleven* (1811). Warrington, Eng.: Sunrise Publishing, 1911.

Bonneville, C. M. Le Roy de. *Étude biographique et littéraire sur Cousin de Grainville*. Le Havre: Imprimerie Lepellettier, 1863.

Brians, Paul. *Nuclear Holocausts: Atomic War in Fiction, 1895–1984*. Kent, Ohio: Kent State University Press, 1987.

Bull, Malcolm. *Apocalypse Theory and the Ends of the World*. Oxford: Blackwell, 1995.

Burdon, Christopher. *The Apocalypse in England: Revelation Unravelling, 1700–1834*. Basingstoke, Eng.: Macmillan, 1997.

Caillens, Pierre. *La Fin du monde en S.F.* Libourne: E. Godeau, 1994.

Carey, Frances, ed. *The Apocalypse and the Shape of Things to Come*. Published to accompany an exhibition at the British Museum, December 1999–April 2000. London: British Museum Press, 1999.

Cioranescu, Alexandre. *L'Avenir du passé: Utopie et littérature*. Paris: Gallimard, 1972.

Clarke, I. F. *The Pattern of Expectation, 1644–2001*. London: Cape, 1979.

———. *Voices Prophesying War*. Oxford: Oxford University Press, 1992.

Delumeau, Jean. *Mille ans de bonheur.* Paris: Fayard, 1995.

Gillispie, Charles Coulston. *The Montgolfier Brothers and the Invention of Aviation.* Princeton: Princeton University Press, 1983.

Goldstein, Laurence. *Ruins and Empires: The Evolution of a Theme in Augustan and Romantic Literature.* Pittsburgh: University of Pittsburgh Press, 1977.

Grainville, Jean-Baptiste François Xavier Cousin de. *Le Dernier Homme.* Paris: Deterville, 1805.

——. *Le Dernier Homme.* 2d ed. Edited by Charles Nodier. Paris: Ferra et Deterville, 1811.

——. *Le Dernier Homme.* Geneva: Slatkine Reprints, 1976.

——. *The Last Man; or, Omegarus and Syderia: A Romance in Futurity.* London: R. Dutton, 1806.

——. *The Last Man; or, Omegarus and Syderia.* New York: Arno Press, 1978.

Krishan, Kumar. *Utopia and Anti-Utopia in Modern Times.* Oxford: Blackwell, 1991.

Macaulay, Rosemary. *The Pleasure of Ruins.* London: Thames and Hudson, 1977.

Michelet, Jules. *Histoire du XIXe siècle jusqu'à Waterloo.* 3 vols. Paris: Michel Lévy Frères, 1875.

O'Neil, H. *Two Thousand Years Hence.* London: Chapman and Hall, 1867.

Patrides, C. A., and Joseph Wittreich, eds. *The Apocalypse in English Renaissance Thought and Literature.* Ithaca, N.Y.: Cornell University Press, 1984.

The Reign of George VI, 1900–1925 (1763). Edited by I. F. Clarke. London: Cornmarket Reprints, 1972.

Roche, Eugenius. *London in a Thousand Years.* London: Colburn and Bentley, 1830.

Sandison, Alan, and Robert Dingley. *Histories of the Future: Studies in Fact, Fantasy and Science Fiction.* Basingstoke, Eng.: Palgrave, 2000.

Seed, David, ed. *American Science Fiction and the Cold War.* Edinburgh: Edinburgh University Press, 1999.

———. *Imagining Apocalypse: Studies in Cultural Crisis.* New York and Basingstoke: St. Martin's Press and Macmillan Press, 2000.

Shelley, Mary. *The Last Man* (1826). Edited with an introduction and notes by Morton D. Paley. Oxford: Oxford World's Classics, 1998.

Shiel, M. P. *The Purple Cloud* (1901). Aylesbury, Eng.: Panther Books, 1969.

Smith, Horace. *Poetical Works.* London: Henry Colburn, 1846.

Stafford, Fiona J. *The Last of the Race: The Growth of a Myth from Milton to Darwin.* Oxford: Clarendon Press, 1933.

Thompson, L. L. *The Book of Revelation: Apocalypse and Empire.* New York: Oxford University Press, 1990.

Touroude, Alfred. *Les Écrivains havrais.* Le Havre: Librairie de E. Touroude, 1865.

Tuveson, Ernest L. *Millennium and Utopia: A Study in the Background of the Idea of Progress.* Berkeley: University of California Press, 1949.

Versins, Pierre. *Encyclopédie de l'Utopie, des Voyages extraordinaires, et de la Science-Fiction.* Lausanne: L'Age d'Homme, 1972.

Vidal, Gore. *Kalki.* London: Heinemann, 1978.

Volney, Constantin-François. *Les Ruines, ou Méditations sur les révolutions des empires.* Paris: Desenne, Vollan, Plassan, 1792.

Wagar, W. Warren. *Terminal Visions: The Literature of Last Things.* Bloomington: Indiana University Press, 1982.

Wells, H. G. *The Time Machine* (1895). Edited by Frank D. McConnell. New York: Oxford University Press, 1977.

Wilkie, Everett C. "Mercier's *L'An 2440,* Part I." *Harvard Library Bulletin* 32 (winter 1984): 5–35.

———. "Mercier's *L'An 2440,* Part II: Bibliography." *Harvard Library Bulletin* 32 (fall 1984): 349–400.

Woodhead, Christopher. *In Ruins.* London: Chatto and Windus, 2001.

Library of Congress Cataloging-in-Publication Data

Cousin de Grainville, Jean-Baptiste-François-Xavier, 1746–1805.

[Dernier homme. English]

The last man / Jean-Baptiste-François-Xavier Cousin

de Grainville ; translated by I. F. & M. Clarke ;

introduction & critical material by I. F. Clarke.

   p. cm. — (Wesleyan early classics of science fiction series)

Includes bibliographical references.

ISBN 0-8195-6549-0 (cloth : alk. paper) —

ISBN 0-8195-6608-x (pbk. : alk. paper)

I. Clarke, I. F. (Ignatius Frederick) II. Clarke, M. (Margaret), 1928–

III. Title. IV. Series.

PQ1987.G13 D413 2002

843'.6—dc21   2002029909